Bob Moats

I0538886

Sin City Murders

1

Sin City Murders

This book is licensed for your personal use only. This book may not be re-sold or given away to other people. If you would like to share this book with another person, please purchase an additional copy for each recipient. If you're reading this book and did not purchase it, or it was not purchased for your use only, please purchase your own copy. Thank you for respecting the hard work of this author.

ISBN -978-0-9960845-7-4

For information and address:
Magic 1 Productions
P.O. Box 524, Fraser MI 48026-0524
Website: http://murdernovels.com
Cover by Bob Moats
Photo from Fotosearch.com

Bob Moats

Other Jim Richards series books by Bob Moats

For a preview or to purchase a book, go to
http://murdernovels.com

What a few people are saying about Murder Novels by Bob Moats

Mr. Moats, I just got your novel "Classmate Murders" and have to let you know, I read it in one evening. That is the first book I have ever done that with. That was the most enjoyable book I have ever read. I just started reading e-books, and reading again, after getting my wife a Kindle. This book was my 12th, and the best. I just got Las Vegas Showgirls to (read) tomorrow evening. I look forward to reading many of your books in this series. I have been searching for an author and books that were fun, entertaining reads. Your books are just the ticket.

Regards, A new fan, Bill from South Carolina

****

Another very nice comment submitted through my website from Micki P.:

"I recently was given a kindle for my 60th birthday. The first book I downloaded was the Classmate Murders and have now read every one of the them. Today I started on the Fatal Rejection series. Thank you for the wonderful ride with Jim and Penny and all the rest of the troop. I have laughed and giggled thru the stories, my poor family gave me the strangest looks! Now I really want a little Yorkie!! Fatal Rejection so far is another great read! I will be looking out for more of Jim Richards and since you are my #1 Author, anything of yours I can find."

Extra special thanks to:

My gratitude to Sally Berneathy who edited this book and is editing my other books. If you need an editor for your work go to http://sallyberneathy.com for more info.

Thank you for purchasing this book. I hope you enjoy it as much as I enjoyed writing it for my faithful readers. Please feel free to email me to tell me what you thought about my stories. I can be reached at murdernovels@bobmoats.com thanks again!

The Jim Richards Family of Readers is listed in the back of the book.

Sin City Murders by Bob Moats

Chapter 1

The woman stood at the edge of the Stratosphere tower looking out over the Las Vegas valley. From her vantage point she had a real nice view of the city, and all its people moving around like ants. Of course being almost a thousand feet in the air helped to make the people look like ants and right now the woman could care less about all those people. At that moment she was more concerned about how she would look after she hit the ground below. Maybe this wasn't the best way to kill one's self. She thought about going back in the building and maybe buying some rat poison and do herself in that way. But what if she didn't take the right amount? She'd end up getting her stomach pumped and being put away for observation to see if she was stable enough to be let loose again. She hated the institution she had just gotten out of; she had been there because she had tried to slit her wrists, which she botched.

Okay, jumping off the tallest structure west of the Mississippi was something that even she couldn't botch on her own, so this was the way to do it. She looked down, something she shouldn't have done, but took a huge breath and did a beautiful Swan dive out from the footing. Her body floated downward being pummeled around a bit by the high winds that came across the valley every so often, to make life miserable for the city. She was now floating over towards the busy Las Vegas Boulevard below, instead of the parking lot she had hoped to hit. As she watched the ground below coming up in seemingly slow motion, she wondered what points of her life would flash before her eyes. She wanted to re-live a few things that she had enjoyed in her miserable life.

Her body was now directly over the busy boulevard of tourist cars going on their way to gamble or watch an expensive show. She didn't care, she just wanted to die. By the time she had made impact, a household furniture moving truck had pulled up below her. She crashed through the top of the cargo portion into a pile of mattresses that barely cushioned her fall. She was not in good shape, but she also wasn't dead, she lay there hurting badly and just mumbled, "Crap!"

~~*~~

Sin City Murders

Penny had already started to plan on decorating the home we purchased just on the west edge of the city of Las Vegas. The home had this fantastic view of the entire Vegas strip, all it's casinos and hotels standing tall, and the mountains looming up behind the strip. We were almost on the foot of the mountains behind us; we had a good sized backyard but since it started to go upwards to the high cliffs behind us, we had no great view back there, but it was private. The wall of rock also provided a natural fence so we couldn't be attacked by pirates from the rear, unless they rappelled down the face of the mountain. Willy, our pet toy Yorkie, was loving the large area to run, it was peaceful and fairly secluded. The next neighbor to us was about a city block away on the long, winding road that led over to Mt. Charleston. We were a bit out of the way from the city, but it would be nice because of the seclusion.

Our good friends, and a couple of Las Vegas Metro Police's finest detectives, Deacon and Lynn had been busy helping us take stuff from the moving truck into the house. I had paid my son to drive the moving truck out from Michigan, with my Crown Vic being towed behind and he helped with unloading the truck also. He saved me from having to strain my back.

Bob Moats

Penny and I had driven back out to Vegas in the Lincoln mini-limo that I had received from the Traviano Mob family in New York for saving their niece, and the trip took us just four days of travel which was nice being in the comfortable car. We had gone back to Michigan to sort out our lives and bring back with us just what we needed. I left Earl Daws in charge of the Michigan office of my investigation firm, he did hint that he may move out to Vegas one day also. Penny and I decided to let my son, his wife and our grandson move into the Michigan house while we were out in Vegas, until next summer when we would go back to stay a couple weeks with the family for a visit. My daughter-in-law and grandson were presently staying in the house until my son went back, so the house wasn't unattended. After we had emptied the moving truck, we took it to the nearest U-Haul rental place to drop off, then we drove my son to the airport and he flew back, being picked up at Metro Airport in Detroit by my brother.

My friend and business partner Buck had decided since everyone was deserting him, and with coaxing from Deacon's sister Maria, he would also move, but keeping his house and options open for going back. He had his brother help him pack a small moving truck and towed his classic T-Bird in back. He wanted the car with him in Vegas to be able to really enjoy his "ride".

Penny and Lynn had made a number of shopping trips to the huge mall not far from us, another factor in Penny's decision that we buy the house. They made a number of trips in Deacon's big Chevy truck and then I was finally asked to go with Penny to pick out some furniture. We found a nice store on Lynn's recommendation and bought a houseful of furniture, to be delivered in the next two days or it would be free. I'd like to see them make good on that promise, the furniture cost a fortune.

The house was now taking on a little shape, Penny had bought curtains and we spent a couple hours putting them up. Deacon was handy since he was taller than all of us, so he had the job of putting up the hardware for the curtains. We manage to cover the front of the house to keep prying eyes out, but I doubted there would be many eyes out here. Penny was like me when it came to windows being uncovered at night, we liked the curtains closed.

It was just before night fall and we all sat in the front yard watching the sun's light slowly move up the mountains across from us as the sun set behind our mountain. The lights of Vegas were just coming on in full force and it was a beauty to behold. The beam of light from the Luxor had been turned on and I remembered our first trip out here when I was shot and I hallucinated that I sat on the top of the pyramid.

"So without bedroom furniture, where you two going to sleep tonight?" Deacon asked as he laid back on the chaise lounge Penny and Lynn had dragged home from Wal-Mart along with the rest of the lawn chairs they could get in the truck.

"We're camping out. I had our gear thrown in the moving truck from Michigan and we are pitching the tent and rolling out the sleeping bag." I replied as Penny smiled next to me. "The camping stuff will come in handy as we plan on camping a lot up on Mt. Charleston."

"It's going to be cold tonight." Deacon warned, "It's still winter here you know, and at night the temperature can drop in the low thirties."

"We're camping in the living room, so we'll be warm and toasty with a roaring fire in the fireplace." I answered.

Lynn's cell phone rang and she answered, listened for a minute then hung up smiling widely. "Want to hear something really different?"

We all waited for her to speak, "It seems a woman took a nose dive off the Stratosphere and landed in a truckload of mattresses. She lived and is mostly stunned, she's lucky. The big deal was she left a suicide note saying she was killing herself because she couldn't stand the nightmares from a murder she thinks she committed. She's not in shape to explain tonight so I've been assigned to go talk to her if she comes around tomorrow."

Penny looked to me and mumbled, "Murder rears its ugly head again, don't even think about going near her or you'll sleep out with the rocks."

I laughed and said I'd stay away. I looked down the road and could see Buck coming up in his T-Bird with Maria, and after they parked the two of them came over to us with a magnum of champagne. "A little house warming gift." He grinned. I thanked him and said we didn't have any glasses yet. Penny said to hold on and went into the house coming back out with a box of glassware she had bought earlier today on one of her shopping trips with Lynn. She opened the box and handed me the first glass after I popped the cork off the bottle. I poured the liquid and handed them out to everyone. Buck had his small bottle of Sprite and we toasted.

"To good friends, good house, good weather, good life, good night," and I drank.

After it was finally dark and the lights of Las Vegas were brilliant on the floor of the valley, along with the beam of light shooting up from the Luxor Pyramid, everyone was tiring so they all left. Penny went into the house and brought a couple more beers from the fridge and we sat relaxing, listening to the night air blowing around the hills. It was a more gentle breeze now, better than the howling winds earlier. We held hands as we sat watching the circus of Sin City moving and glittering before us.

"Why didn't we do this a year ago?" Penny asked.

"I don't think we were ready for it. You had to finally decide to get away from your talk show and I had to get away from my family. It was the right time now and I'm not regretting it at all."

She suddenly stood and kissed me on the top of my bald head. "I'm getting a bit chilly. I think I'll go in and start a fire, care to join me? You can pitch the tent and we can cuddle." She gave me her evil little smile and said, "Then we can christen the house."

She went off into the house with Willy following her, I sat for a moment longer just feeling the atmosphere of the place, I was home now.

**

Chapter 2

I guess it was morning; I was prone on the floor, in the totally silent house. Willy wasn't even licking my face. Penny wasn't either. We had christened the house last night, and then we christened the floor, the walls, the tent, the sleeping bag, the new curtains and any other object we could think of. It was a night of christening our brains out. I sat up realizing I was naked, my clothes were strewn around the floor. I had no idea what time it was, my watch was strewn somewhere around my clothes. I stood carefully, since my back was feeling a slight twinge from the air mattress we slept on. I was used to my bed and this new mattress needed a little more air. Damn I hate getting older.

I had managed to find my BVD's and put them on while I hopped to the kitchen to see where my wife was off to. She wasn't in the kitchen, but the patio door was open off the dining area, so she must be in the backyard I deduced. That's why I'm the private eye, I make these deductions. I went out and could hear water splashing, Penny was in the half-sized Olympic pool we had in the back, just past the ugly fountain that stood in the middle of the courtyard. The fountain came with the house; it was one feature I didn't care for. It was of some Grecian God pouring water from a pitcher into the small circular pond full of koi fish all waiting to be fed. I reached in the can by the feet of the water God and grabbed a handful of pellets, tossing them to the giant goldfish that devoured the feed like piranhas.

I came around to the pool and saw Willy, our toy Yorkie, sitting quietly on a lawn chair shaking. He usually shook when he was excited, frightened or hungry. He shook a lot. But I think he was shaking now, watching Penny swim back and forth in the pool, hoping that he wasn't going to be in the water also. I came over and he saw me, shaking harder now as I sat in the lawn chair next to him, petting his head.

"Don't worry buddy, I'm not going to throw you in. It's the last place I would be myself." I had this thing about water, well, being in water. It was not something I cared for. I watched Penny doing her strokes back and forth then realized she was naked. I almost jumped in with her.

She finally brought her head up and saw me, she waved. I waved back and told Willy to wave to mommy. He didn't. Penny went to the steps coming out of the pool and came bouncing over, literally, to me. She had great breasts that held up very well for a woman a year from being sixty. She picked up the towel from the bench and started to dry off.

"About time you got up, are you feeling okay this morning?" She asked as I studied her body.

"I'm barely alive and barely dressed. How long have you been up?"

"About an hour, I decided to start my day every morning with a swim, since we have it. We need a whirlpool spa now, right over there." she pointed to a bare spot of backyard that just screamed to be fill with a spa.

"I'll call the pool people today and have one brought out, just for you." I replied.

"So, you wouldn't even sit naked with me in a whirlpool. We used to do it back when we stayed at the MGM Grand during the convention, or have you forgotten?"

"I have no problems with being in a whirlpool; I just don't care for deep water that one can drown in. Like the pool." I replied.

"You can't swim can you?" She accused.

"I just have no desire to, or to drown."

"Well, I'm going to teach you, that's an order. I took swim class in school, remember?" She laughed.

"Oh I remember, it was the one area of the school I loved to take pictures, at least that's I told the teachers, I was taking pictures for the yearbook, I lied."

"Well, you are going to learn, and then we can both get up early and go for a nice swim."

I mumbled to Willy, "There's nothing nice about early or a swim."

"What did you say, Sweetie?"

"I said that it would be nice getting up early for a swim." I smiled.

"Yeah, that's what I thought you said." She stuck her tongue out at me and sat on my lap, still naked. "Shall I do a lap dance for you?"

"Have you taken a swing around your new stripper pole yet?" I asked looking to the pole that was embedded in the concrete just off the pool. It was part of this property that was formerly owned by one Brett Wallis, a famous burlesque producer and entertainer. He had a great show running on the strip that I had seen when I worked here. I got to know Brett and a few of the topless dancers from the show since I would get them tickets to see Nick North's show. I thought about the man I had worked for and wondered if Nick was entertaining in prison now. Brett used to have some great parties here and the stripper pole was installed to provide entertainment for his guests. Penny saw the stripper pole when we first came to view the property with the real estate guy, and she knew it was a sign.

"Yes, I did a few maneuvers on it earlier; it's a much better pole than what I had back in Michigan. I like it."

"So did the real estate guy when we came out here and you attacked the pole and did a number of maneuvers around it then. His jaw dropped to his belt."

"Well, between the gigantic mall, the pool and the pole, I just had to live here." She smiled as we heard the property alarm go off. Penny jumped being startled and went to get her robe. I went into the kitchen to the control panel for the security equipment and turned on the TV monitor and saw Deacon and Lynn in the drive. The entire property had sensors installed so if anyone walked onto the property, alarms would sound. The driveway had another alarm to warn if someone drove in. It was a nice system and would let us run around naked until someone invaded us.

I went to the family room and gathered my clothes to dress, by that time Penny had slipped into a jump suit and was at the door greeting our friends.

"We came up behind a furniture truck coming up the road a few miles back, I sped ahead to warn you they were coming." Deacon said just as the truck pulled up to the front of the house, three big men got out and one came to the door. I went to greet them being disappointed that they beat the schedule so my furniture wasn't going to be free. I took the invoice he had and said to start bringing it all in. Penny took command and Lynn fell in behind her to direct the men as to where the furniture would go.

About an hour later, everything was in the house, I gave the men a nice tip and they left. Penny said she had to do some rearranging to make it look better, so we spent another hour moving furniture around so Penny could see where she liked it best. Deacon and I had just finished with moving furniture when Buck and Maria walked in and Buck asked if he could help.

"Good Timing Buck, we just finished." I laughed.

We all sat on the new living room furniture and Lynn told us about the tower diving woman. "The woman, Lacey Lee, was barely awake when I got to the LV Medical Center and she had quite a tale to tell. She said about three months ago she woke in a man's bed at some motel off the north end of the strip, and found the guy dead next to her. She had a knife in her hand and blood all over her. She went to wash the blood off and clean up, she said she was puking in the toilet and must have fallen asleep there. When she woke, she went back out to the room and there was no body or blood. She also said it wasn't even the same room she was in earlier. She claims she had to have been moved. She called the police and they did a look-see of the motel and found nothing. I talked to the primary officer on that case and he told me they found no evidence of foul play or murder in any room of the motel."

"Did she know who the man was?" I asked.

"No, she doesn't even remember going to the motel or where she was. They took her in for psyche evaluation and she was getting really paranoid now. She was having bad dreams about the murder and could see many people in her dream stabbing the man. The hospital she was in said they worked with her for a month then her hospitalization insurance was running low, so they cut her loose."

"Oh sure, just let the insane wander the streets now, that's where most homeless people come from. Patients being turned loose by mental hospitals because they have no money to pay for treatment." Penny grumbled.

"I'm afraid you're very correct about that, most homeless are people who need treatment. But that's a whole other debate. This woman wasn't homeless, she was a dealer at one of the smaller casinos over by Boulder highway. But her health insurance was cut back and she didn't have enough funds to be given further treatment. She said she started having really bad dreams and she had become despondent about the whole incident so she tried to commit suicide by slitting her wrists. Unfortunately, or fortunately, she didn't quite cut her wrists properly for her to bleed out, she missed the vein. She was found by a friend and taken back to the hospital and the whole thing went around again. The woman said she had it with medical people poking and probing her, she wants the police to investigate, but without a crime we could do nothing. That's why she took a nose dive off the Stratosphere. It's sad really."

Penny looked to me, "I see wheels turning, you aren't thinking of looking into this are you?"

"Well, if there was no real murder, how can I not help this poor woman?" I smiled.

**

Chapter 3

Deacon finally spoke, "Well, before you do any investigating, you'll need to get your P.I. license established here in Nevada. I'll help you with the paperwork when I can, just come on down to the precinct and we'll get you set up with a CCW also. Don't carry till we get it all official. I can go with you to talk to the woman if you want, just to make it official for now."

"Thanks Deacon, I appreciate that."

Lynn looked at Penny and said, "If you could have seen her, it was heart wrenching to listen and then check out her story. She seems like a really sweet girl who's wrapped in a mystery and as a cop I can't help her. Maybe Jim can."

"Since you're not doing your show now, you can come along with me to help." I said to Penny hoping that would make it easier to get away with taking the case. She sat there looking like she was deciding to or not.

"Do I get a license too?" She asked.

Everyone laughed and I said, "I'll get you a junior detective badge that you can flash when in trouble."

"All right, it's a deal." She smiled.

We all went out to the backyard and I headed over to the huge barbecue monolith that was off the side of the yard. It was made of adobe bricks and looked like a nuclear reactor. I opened the hood and it was filled with charcoal briquettes that looked just right for burning. I found a can of starter and poured the liquid on, then borrowed a lighter from Lynn, which she said she had for emergencies, and lit the thing. The ball of fire that rose up from the pit was enough to rival the beam of light from the Luxor. I was sure it could be seen from outer space. Penny came to me and asked if I had a permit to operate an incinerator and then said "What are we going to B-B-Q?"

I had a few surprises up my sleeve and went into the house to the huge double door refrigerator and pulled out the container of steaks that I smuggled in yesterday when I went to the store for more beer. I brought them out to the cheers of everyone and Penny said she was going to whip up a side dish. That scared me, but she was a fairly good cook. She and Lynn went into the kitchen as I watched the steaks sizzle on the grill.

As we ate our meal and I commented on wondering what Trapper was up to, I said I'd have to call him. Deacon said he missed Trapper every so often, all the funny things Trapper would pull around the precinct. "Vegas has something going on all the time in the way of crimes, but it's so routine. The last time we had a real laugh was when Trapper and Becker were running around Vegas pulling all those pranks on Captain Weber when you guys were out here for your wedding."

"So you haven't had any real serious crimes or murders since Jim left Vegas that last time?" Penny asked making a stab at my curse.

"Oh, we've had murders, mostly gang bangers or tourists who went into the wrong part of town for a little action, but no serial killers or mass murderers. So, no, we haven't had any real good murders since Jim left." Lynn was in on the joke now.

I picked up my empty paper plate and said, "Fine, you can joke about my predilection for having good crimes to solve, and I usually have a few following me, but I get the job done." I went to the garbage can in the box on the back of the attached garage and dumped my plate. "I plan on starting my P.I. business out here and if I happen to run into a crime that the Vegas police can't handle, so be it."

"Sweetie, you have me now to help solve your crimes, like "McMillan and Wife" with Rock Hudson. We'll be the new husband and wife crime fighters." Penny looked serious when she said it, I just cringed.

We spent the rest of the afternoon just relaxing; Penny, Maria and Lynn decided to spend most of it in the pool. Maria and Lynn fit well into one of Penny's dozens of swimsuits; I had none since I wasn't a pool person. Deacon, Buck and I just sat and watched the women frolic.

Around six everyone was heading out so we walked them to their cars. Deacon said he'd come by tomorrow morning to take Penny and me to the hospital to see Lacey Lee. Penny said she'd be ready, I said I'll try to be up early. After our friends had all left, Penny and I went into our new home to see what we could do with the new furniture.

We sat on the new couch in front of the humongous LCD TV that the men had installed on the wall. Willy was a bit confused by the new furniture and was trying different places to lie down. We had his favorite chair that we brought with us from Michigan but it was in the bedroom. He settled on the new recliner and claimed it for himself.

"We've been out here almost two weeks, mostly staying in Caesar's Palace, but we haven't even gone to any of the shows yet. Now that we are settled a little, let's start taking in all the places we haven't visited in the past." I said.

"I want to see Celine Dion first." Penny asked.

"She left last year, its Cher now. But Celine is coming back I hear."

"Good, that's where I want to go, to see Cher."

"You got it. So what is your take on the tower diving woman?" I asked to see if she was still interested.

"Lynn told me a few more details on her while we relaxed around the pool, I think you'll have something interesting to solve if what I hear is true." She told me very little more than what Lynn had already said, but I gave her my full attention. We sat quietly then I looked to her and said, "Let's go check the new bed, we haven't christened it yet." She grinned and ran off to the bedroom, I followed.

We spent the next morning relaxing on the new mattress admiring the new bed set and talking about what we wanted to do with the furniture in the rest of the house, just as the phone rang. I reached over to the bed stand and answered, it was Deacon.

"Good morning, are you up and raring to go already?" I asked.

"I'm just getting up; I'll pick you guys up around noon, that's when they let cops interrogate patients. I'll see you then." He disconnected and I put the phone back on the base.

"Well, we have a couple of hours to kill, pardon the pun, is there anything else we need to christen?" I said, and then Penny laughed and jumped out of the bed.

"No, not right now, but I'm going to teach you to swim, so get up!" She ordered and I just groaned. "Now or you'll never christen anything in this house again."

I swung my feet over the side and stood begrudgingly; I followed her down to the pool, both of us still naked. We stood at the narrow end of the pool looking down the long body of water. "Now you need to know some things about swimming." She said.

"You mean, like this." I said as I did a dive off the concrete into the pool and did two complete laps in speedy time. I came back to her and bobbed up hanging on to the edge.

"You sorry son-of-a-bitch, no offense to your mother, you can swim!" She yelled down to me.

"Yep, I still hate water but I did learn about two years before we met. It was a challenge I made to myself. So, want to come in and fool around." I reached out and grabbed her leg and pulled her to an off-balance state and she tumbled in. Making love in water is something everyone should try once in their lives, we tried it twice, maybe more.

Around eleven-thirty we were dressed and ready to go. Penny smacked my behind and said I was a bad boy for not telling her I could swim. I said I was waiting for a good time to rescue her from drowning to show off my swimming skills. She asked where I practiced after the lessons; I said I would go to the YMCA in Mt. Clemens. She just made a face and said I was still a bad boy and would be punished severely. I couldn't wait.

Sin City Murders

Just before noon, Deacon pulled in setting off the driveway alarm, and Penny and I went out to greet him. We drove over to LV Medical Center and parked. We headed up to the floor where Lacey Lee was at and started to go into her room just as a nurse asked what we were doing and Deacon flashed his badge and said police business. She smiled and said Miss Lee was awake. We entered the room and found her sitting up eating from a tray, it didn't look appetizing.

She looked up and her eyes got wide, "Hey, you're that lady from the TV, what's her name, Martha Stewart?"

Penny laughed and said, "No, I'm Penny Wickens."

"Oh, yeah, that's it, the talk show lady on the CW. I know you now."

Penny went to her bedside and said, "I'm not doing the show anymore, I've retired and living here in Vegas."

"Wow, and you're here to see me. I know the big guy, he's a cop, but who's the old guy?" She asked. I was offended.

Penny got a big laugh out of that, "He's my husband, Jim Richards. He's a private investigator."

"Oh, yeah. You're the one from that TV movie about the killers of the cheerleaders. You solved that case."

28

I went to the bed and said, "Yes I did; now I want to help solve your case."

**

Chapter 4

The woman was more of a girl, barely 23 and acted like a teenager, kind of a bubblehead. She was cute and had a voice that reminded me of one of those mice in the Tom and Jerry cartoons, high and squeaky.

"Miss Lee, I'm going to try to help you find out what happened that night you say the murder occurred. But I will need your full cooperation if I'm to help. Can you do that?" I asked.

She thought for a couple of seconds and said she would. "Wow, a famous TV lady and her detective husband, I'm psyched. Are you going to investigate too?" She asked of Penny.

"Yes, I'm going to help." Penny laughed and pulled a chair over, placing it next to the bed and sat, taking Lacey's hand she asked, "Lacey why don't you tell us about yourself?" I thought Penny was going to interview her like she did on her show, which wasn't a bad idea. It would make the girl relax and be more receptive to our questions.

"Sure, I was born here in Vegas and lived with my parents until they divorced when I was five. I lived with my mother since my dad had a gambling problem and never had enough money to take care of me let alone pay child support to my Mom. I had to start working early to help with bills. I worked for an uncle of my mom's, he's a pit boss at the Silver Dust casino, it's a small casino over on Boulder Highway. I've worked there for four years now, it helped take care of my mom, but she passed away last year from cancer." She paused and looked like a tear was forming in her eyes; Penny grabbed a tissue from the stand next to the bed and said to take her time.

"Thanks, the house we lived in was paid for by her uncle and he let me live there after my mom passed, I still do." She smiled now and Penny asked, "Moving up to the night just before you woke in the motel room, do you remember what happened?"

"That was a crazy night, I remember getting off work at the casino around ten in the evening and then going into the lounge to have a couple quick drinks, just to relax, then I went out to the employee parking and got my car. I drove out Boulder Highway going to the freeway to go home but I felt a tire starting to go flat. I don't know how to change a tire, so I pulled into a parking lot of a closed auto parts place and stopped the car. Right behind me was this big SUV and there was this guy in it. He got out and asked if I needed help. Well, duh! I told him I didn't know how to change a tire, he said he would if I could just open the trunk. I did and he started to change it for me. He was on the ground putting the tire on when he stopped to unwrap one of those round Dum-Dum suckers on a stick, he asked if I wanted one. My mother always told me never take candy from a stranger, but he was so nice to help, so I took one. I unwrapped it and put it in my mouth but after a while it tasted funny. That was the last thing I remember."

Penny looked to me, I looked to Deacon. He said, "When they investigated Miss Lee's claim of the incident, the primary officer took his men to the parts store and after searching the parking lot they found a sucker stick on the ground. Forensics said it had been laced with a fast acting sedative. The store owner pointed out her car saying it was just parked in the middle of the lot when he came in that morning; he had his employees move it to the side. CSI was called and dusted the car but found no prints other than Miss Lee's and a few from the store employees."

"Yes, I remember, he wore gloves the whole time he worked on the car." Lacey offered.

I looked to Deacon and asked, "Has she given a description to a sketch artist?"

"Yes she did," he said as he brought up the manila envelope he was carrying and took out a copy of the sketch. He handed it to me; I showed it to Penny then turned it towards the girl. "Was this the man who changed your tire?"

"That was him or as close to him as I could remember."

"Was this also the man you found murdered in bed the next morning?"

"No he wasn't, I really didn't get a good look at the dead man's face but he wasn't the same guy. I was so shocked by all the blood and the body; I just looked briefly at him then went to the bathroom to throw up. I was in the bathroom the whole time until I woke up on the toilet and I was somewhere else."

"How did you know you were someplace else?"

"The room was different. The walls were brighter and the door was on the right instead of the left. I know because I looked to the door to see where I could get out. The bed was all made and clean, no blood anywhere in the place."

The door to the room opened and the nurse came in explaining she had some routine checks to do on the patient. Penny moved so the nurse could get to Lacey. We stood back while the nurse did the usual blood pressure and temperature checks.

I turned to Deacon and asked if she was going to be released anytime soon, he said he'd ask. "I'd like to revisit the motel and take her along to see if there's anything that may jog her memory. How much did the primary officer investigate on this?"

"There was no murder crime scene, the drugging was about the only thing they really went into as a possible kidnap and rape, but the rape kit came up negative. So they didn't focus on it much. According to Detective Mason, the investigating officer assigned, they had a ton of other caseloads to take care of and this girl wasn't a high priority. Mason treated her like a hooker who had a bad night with a john."

Penny said, "That's tragic, this girl needed more attention than just a brush off."

"I know Penny, but sometimes even the best cops are jerks. I don't excuse it, but it happens." Deacon offered.

"Well we are going to help this girl. Aren't we Sherlock?" she smiled to me.

The nurse finished and Deacon asked her how long before she would be discharged. The nurse asked him to step out of the room; I followed as Penny went back to Lacey.

"Uh, Detective, the patient is going to be transferred to the psyche ward for evaluation due to her suicide attempt. You'll have to talk to Dr. Stevens about this. I brought you out here to tell you so not to upset her." The nurse smiled and went off to do her job elsewhere.

"I wonder if we can bust her out of here and get away with it." I said.

"I'll have a talk with this doctor and see if we can place her in protective custody on suicide watch. It's worked before, may work this time, especially if we can help her to get over the ordeal." Deacon said. I thanked him and we went back in the room.

Penny was talking to her as we came up, she turned to me and smiled, "We were just making small talk. She was asking me about a few celebrities I had on my show."

"We are going to see if we can get you released and go back to the motel to start from there. Would that be alright with you?"

"They aren't going to take me back to the nut hatch?" she asked.

"We're going to see if we can avoid that, but we may have to tell them we will assume responsibility for you, so you'd have to do what we say, is that going to be a problem?"

"I have no problem with it, I can't seem to take care of myself, it will be nice to have people worry about me." She finally smiled.

"All right, we'll be back when we can get you out of here, so hang in there. Sorry, I didn't mean it like that." I said remembering her dive off the tower.

She actually laughed, probably from the wave of relief, "I was stupid for that stunt, but I was hurting too. I mean hurting before the jump, well, it was more of a bigger hurt after. Did you ever face death from a thousand feet up?"

I went to the side of the bed, sat on the edge and told her about my near dive off the Stratosphere back during the showgirl murders when someone tried to push me off the tower. "Yep, I looked down that same drop you did, but I hung on for dear life, I didn't want to fall. I have to say I admire you for the guts that it took to do it, but it was foolish."

She was quiet and said, "I have lived in terror since the day I woke in that room. The dreams kept coming and I couldn't get anyone to help make them go away, I was getting desperate. I had this hole in my life and it was terrifying me. Please help me."

I stood and said, "We will, just put some faith in us. We'll do our best, and stay away from the roof." She laughed, it sounded good.

**

Chapter 5

Deacon asked the nurse where we could find Dr. Stevens, she gave us directions to his office and we headed that way. We found the door with his name painted on it and entered. There was a secretary typing at a small desk and Deacon asked if Dr. Stevens was in, flashing his badge. She squinted to read the shield.

"You're lucky, he just came in. Shall I say what it's about?" She did her job well.

"It's about a patient. We need to talk to the doctor about getting her released." Deacon said.

"One moment please." She picked up her phone and made a call. She hung up, then a door off the side of the room opened and out came a smallish, round man, no hair, pointy nose, bulging eyes, he reminded me of Uncle Fester from the Addams Family.

"May I help you?" He asked, then saw Penny and said, "Aren't you that woman from the TV?" I thought having Penny around didn't hurt, it loosened people up.

Penny smiled and said she was, holding out her hand to shake his and pulling him near enough until she was almost touching his body. I could see he was enjoying it and I figured Penny knew how to work people. I tried not to laugh.

Penny said, "Dr. Stevens, we have a dilemma. This tall gentleman is Detective Frank DeAngelo, with LVMPD, but you can call him Deacon. The other man is my husband, the famous private investigator, Jim Richards. You may have seen the mini-series, Classmate Murders; he lived it and wrote it. Now we need to ask you a favor." He was looking so distracted now, looking into Penny's eyes he would have agreed to free surgery.

Deacon came forward to make the request official, "Dr. Stevens, you have a recently admitted patient who we need to have released to help her solve a murder she thinks she has committed."

"Ah, Miss Lee. Yes, she is a hard case for her two suicide attempts. She has a deep rooted psychosis about the supposed murder, which hasn't been proven yet. But how do you think you can help her if we haven't been able to?"

I spoke now, "Dr. Stevens, we are going to help her by solving the problem that is tormenting her. You and your staff work from in her mind but we will work to bring her the closure she needs to stop the nightmares. We want to find out what happened that night. But we can't do that if she is in this place, we need to take her back and help us."

The doctor stared at me for a moment, "You're the guy who caught the two psychopath serial killers in Michigan aren't you?"

I looked to Deacon and then said, "Yes, I was one of the people who solved that case. In fact, Detective DeAngelo here helped on that also. Now we need to have Miss Lee released when she is physically able, but you want her to go for psychiatric testing. So there is a problem."

"Well, she needs competent care to help her with her mental state." He grinned.

I decided to try a small lie, "Well, her insurance is getting really low, will you help her here pro-bono?"

He stood staring again, and then said, "I think we can work out a release date for her as long as her body is strong enough to carry her out of here and you take responsibility for her." He smiled, I smiled and we shook hands. He said he'd check her to see if she is well enough to travel and we could take her. He excused himself and went out.

I laughed and turned to my companions and said, "Shall we go get our little ward?" We went back to Lacey's room and found the good doctor checking her over and telling the nurse that she was ready to be released. The nurse looked concerned but did what the doctor told her to do.

I took Penny aside and said, "Would it be a problem to let her stay with us in the guest house, till we know the situation?"

"Oh hell no, it won't be a problem, in fact I was going to suggest it myself." She kissed me and we went back to Lacey's bedside now as she was getting dressed by the nurse. She was still hurting from the fall into the mound of mattresses that saved her, but she was feeling better. After a bit of paperwork, she was put in a wheelchair and we pushed her to the lobby while Deacon went to get his car. I asked if they had an extra wheelchair that we could use and the nurse who had to accompany her to the door smiled and said we could take this one. As long as we brought it back. I said we'd get a new one and bring it back as soon as possible.

Lacey was helped into the car and the wheelchair was folded and put in the trunk.

Deacon drove us back to our home and Lacey was amazed by the view we had from the front of the house.

"Lacey, do you swim?" Penny asked. God, she was going to get everyone into that pool I thought. "It will be good for your therapy by being in the pool; it helps you with motor skills, the healing ability of hydrotherapy is well documented, and reduces impact on the body, allowing for better exercise without stressing the body." I looked at my little doctor and smiled. Lacey said she loved to swim; she had a small pool at the house she was living in. That brightened Penny up.

We pushed Lacey to the guest house just off the side of our house and took her in. It was mostly one room with a kitchenette and a separate bath. It was a pleasant room, bright colors and lots of windows that faced the view of the valley. She said she loved it and we got her out of the wheel chair and she stood for a moment, and then got a bit dizzy, so we sat her in an easy chair by a small coffee table. "I'm sorry, but I haven't stood much since the fall. I'll be all right in a while."

Deacon came in, said he had to go back to the precinct and asked if we needed anything else. I thanked him and said no, but to come back when he could with Lynn so we can plot out our attack on this case. I may need some advice. Deacon said he called a friend in licensing and he'd have my paperwork ready to get my P.I. license set up for here. He explained that I would have to retake the qualifying gun test to get my CCW, but it was nothing, just fire at a target, as long as I hit the thing they would pass me. He said he would call later to set up a time, I said I would be ready. He left after saying good-bye to Lacey; she shook his hand and thanked him.

The temperature outside was still in the low seventies, a nice comfortable temperature for winter in Vegas. Penny had opened a couple windows of the guest house to let some air in. Lacey was trying to stand; I helped her and told to take her time.

"I don't want to be a burden on you; it was so nice of you to want to help. I don't know if I can repay you for doing this, I don't have a lot of money."

Penny came over to help her walk a bit. "You are no burden on us, and forget paying us; we do this because we like to help people. Don't we Sweetie?" she said to me.

"Yep, we just enjoy the chase, as long as no one gets hurt." I smiled.

"You said you have a pool?" she asked looking like a child wanting an ice cream.

"Yes we do, I think it wouldn't hurt to get a little swim time in, if you think you can handle it." Penny said happily, I knew she and Lacey would get along well. Penny said she would go in and see if she had a smaller swimsuit and she went off. Lacey spent a short time walking around the room, getting her bearings as I steadied her.

"Lacey, I think we'll take it a little at a time, you just get settled in and then we can go over the details of your ordeal." I offered.

"Thank you, I appreciate it. The police were so rude back when this all happened, they think I was hooking and things went bad. I wasn't honestly; I'd never prostitute myself for anyone."

"I'm sure you wouldn't, so enjoy the swim, get better and then we'll get into the case." I looked to the door when I heard something moving, it was Willy.

He ran in just before Penny came in and he went straight to Lacey bouncing around her feet. She was amazed by the tiny dog and squealed in delight picking up Willy as he wiggled to lick her.

"I think Willy is pissed that we left him here alone, but it wouldn't be a good idea to take him to the hospital, too many bad diseases floating around there." Penny explained to Lacey and held up a couple swimsuits for her. I asked if she was going to bring out her million swimsuits to show Lacey, Penny gave me a dirty look, I excused myself while they did their thing and went out.

I went to the back room of the main house that I claimed as my office, where I was setting up a place to write, work on my computers and any other hobby I might want to indulge in. Penny had a room also where she could do her thing, but she hadn't decided what that would be yet so her room was still empty. I already had computer desks and my computers set up and one nice office desk to hold my laptop for my book writing. The window in my room looked out on the backyard, with a good view of the pool and stripper pole, so I could enjoy whoever was lounging around there. I sat at my desk and brought the laptop out of sleep mode and turned to the internet. I thought maybe there was something about this case that made it to the web. I brought up Google and typed in Lacey's name, but nothing came up for her story.

I looked out my window and saw Penny wheeling Lacey in the chair to the pool. I got up and went out the door from my office that opened to the backyard to see if they needed me. Penny helped Lacey to stand and she walked slowly to the pool's edge and made a beautiful dive into the still water; her dive barely made a ripple in the water, and then she came back up looking like a happy child.

**

Chapter 6

Penny took a dive into the pool. She was wearing a one piece suit, I hoped for a tiny bikini but she was being modest for our guest, I guess. I sat on one of the plastic lawn chairs and watched the two of them swimming around in the cool looking water. Lacey seemed to be getting some strength back to her legs and arms. I can imagine when she hit the truck; it must have been a shock to her body to stop abruptly from the 130 story fall. She was one of those really lucky people who fell from great heights and survive. I remember reading about some guy whose parachute didn't open and he hit the pavement of the airfield, getting up with only a few bruises; amazing.

Penny got out of the water and came over to me, plopping down her wet body on my lap. I winced but she felt good all wet and slippery. She kissed my nose and said, "You want to come in?"

She knew my answer, but I said I may try it later when it warmed up a bit more. I asked if she had turned on the water heater and she called me a wussy. I defended myself saying it was winter and I didn't want to freeze. She looked behind me, on the side of the house was a huge round thermometer and said, "The temperature is now at eighty-two, you'll hardly freeze." She got up and dove back into the pool making a big splash that had me running. Willy was hiding under another lawn chair, shaking as usual. I called him a coward worse than I and sat back down next to his chair. He came over and wanted up so I put him on my lap and we watched the girls play.

Lunch time rolled around and I pulled out some pre-made burger patties and hot dogs and fired up the incinerator as we now called it. I grilled the dogs and burgers while Penny finished the potato salad she had started last night. Lacey was sitting, wrapped in a big towel, holding Willy on her lap. They both looked very contented.

We had just sat down with our food at the picnic table next to the pool, when the driveway alarm went off. Lacey about went out of her skin when it sounded; Penny explained what it was. Lacey said it reminded her of an alarm that went off when she was a child and a fire had started in her home. They got out safely, but half of the house was destroyed. I was at the monitor and could see Buck in the driveway. I called through the intercom and told him to come around the back. He did.

Sin City Murders

I introduced him to Lacey and explained why she was here. He grinned and said he read about her dive off the Stratosphere in the papers, she blushed.

"You are one fortunate young lady," Buck said in his charming way. He asked if there was any help he could give while we were on the case, he said he was getting bored sitting around while Maria was off rehearsing or working at the Tropicana.

"What about your idea to start a guard service?" I asked. He looked to me and smiled.

"I was hoping you were still interested in that. I have been making some inquiries about places to guard. It seems there are a number of places in the north area around where Maria and I are living that would need my services."

Lacey spoke, "If you're talking about North Vegas, there's usually enough crime there from the gangs and the junkies to keep a guard service going nicely."

Buck looked to her and asked, "You know anything about security guard services in that area?"

"Well, I have a friend who used to work for Retcho Guard Service and he had to guard a party store there. It was a dangerous job but he was big and didn't take crap from anyone." She replied.

"Does he still work for them?" Buck asked.

"He got into an argument with the owners over them wanting to cut his hours. He didn't like them anyways, so he quit."

Buck took a business card from his pocket, for our P.I. firm, it had his cell phone number on it and asked, "Have him call me, I'd like to see what the climate is for another guard service."

"There's always room for more guards, you have the gamblers who go broke and rob gas stations to the junkies who need quick cash for a fix, there's enough crime for everyone." she responded.

Buck looked to me and smiled. I said, "You may have started something. Deacon is going to get me all official with my license here, and then I think we need to look for a nice office somewhere to set up our businesses in, my investigating and your guarding."

"I like." Buck grinned and then we cleaned up the mess we made on the table and went inside. Penny was showing Lacey around the house, since Lacey seemed to be getting her bearings back now and was walking better. Penny came to us a few minutes later as Buck and I sat at the snack bar talking business, she said, "I'm taking Lacey to her house to get some clothes and women things, we'll be back shortly." They went out; Penny took the new car we bought for her since we left hers back in Michigan for my son to use.

"Is this girl paying you to help her or is this another charity case?" Buck laughed.

"Hey, I like to help people, and Penny is all for it, so we investigate. Besides it's something to keep my hand back into doing my job. So how's your love life?" I asked changing the subject.

"Maria and I are doing good; we get along well, and have the same tastes. She babies me to the point of being nauseating but I'll survive. Penny still putting up with you?"

"We wouldn't be here if we weren't getting along, now would we?"

"Well I'm sure she is hanging on to you because she wants your insurance money when you croak."

"Hey, I told you that in confidence, you better not tell her about it." I warned.

"I would never tell her that she would be a millionaire if you walked in front of a bus." He snickered.

I got up and went to get the Las Vegas Review-Journal newspaper from the couch and brought it back to the snack counter and opened it to the classifieds. I skimmed down the listings of business offices for rent then Buck and I circled the ones that sounded good. I took out my map of Vegas and we checked the locations of a few that had decent rent and I wrote down the numbers to call, then I put the paper away. My cell phone rang and it was Deacon.

"What's up super cop?" I asked.

"I got you a quick appointment if you can get down here fast to fill out the paper work to establish your Michigan investigators license for use in Nevada." He said.

"Where do I go?" I asked and he gave me directions and I told him we would be there shortly.

I wrote a post-it note to Penny and put it on the front door. Buck and I went to my Crown Vic and we drove into the city up to the county building and found Deacon waiting at the front door.

"That didn't take you long, did you speed?" He asked.

"No I was lucky with the traffic. Now what do I do?"

He took us into the office of licensing and was greeted by a fairly attractive older woman at the counter. "Francis, how are you today."

"I'm fine and don't call me Francis, please." He turned red.

"Well, Lynn calls you that." She replied.

"Yes, when she's pissed at me. Are you pissed at me, Mary?" He asked.

"No, Deacon, I'm not. Now, is this the famous P.I. from Michigan?"

"Yeah, if you can finish the papers so he can be authorized to help a girl to find out if she murdered someone." He said.

She looked at him, then to me and asked, "Does this have something to do with the girl who took a dive off the tower?"

I smiled and said, "You're very observant."

"I've worked around cops way too long. Now let's get you official." She pulled out a small pile of papers and we worked on them for about a half hour. I showed her my Michigan P.I. license and she made a copy of it. She did a few official stampings on the papers and said, "I have to fax this to the Nevada Office of the Attorney General for approval, but don't worry, they hate the paperwork, so they will just rubber stamp my papers and your new license will be mailed to you this week, this is a temp for you to show that it's in the works, but hang on to your Michigan licence if needed."

I thanked her, and she said, "I hope you can help the girl, I read the story and the word is she got a raw deal from the cops on the job. It's a thankless job and sometimes victims fall through the cracks. Good Luck."

I thanked her and then Deacon took us to another building where we met with the LV police armorer and he gave me a routine test, firing a couple hand guns at targets and then he pulled a paper, filled it out, handing it to me and said, "Don't shoot yourself or Deacon. I need him for poker night." He laughed and I thanked him. He said to be sure to register any handguns I may carry, I said I would. While we were there we also took care of Buck's CCW, so he could continue to carry for his guard service.

As we went back to the cars, I said to Deacon, "You're pretty popular around here."

"It's my pretty face and my gigantic body. I either win people over or crush them." He laughed and asked us how it was going with Lacey.

"Penny and she are getting along great. Buck and I are plotting to find an office to start out, so if you know of a place let me know."

He grinned and said to follow him. He went to his car while Buck and I got in my car and followed him out Tropicana again, over the freeway just past the strip and then turned left on Industrial Road, going down a short distance then into an office plaza with a west side view of the back of the huge casinos and hotels of the strip, it looked really nice. He took us into a small office and there was a man at a desk who stood as we came in.

"Deacon, my man, how's it going?" the man spoke loudly.

"I'm good Larry; I need an office, cheap, lots of room, cheap, good view of the city, cheap." Deacon said and introduced us.

"So you want a cheap office but prime everything, what do I look like, a genie?" Larry smirked.

"Larry, you owe me big time, I'm calling in my marker. My goods friends Jim and Buck needs an office and you got too many sitting vacant. So we're making our wish, make it so genie."

Larry stood for a moment, "I got just what you're looking for. I'll take you there." He got a set of keys from his desk and then took us out to the front of the long row of storefront offices, mostly empty. We got to one and he opened the door and we went in. He showed us around and I looked out the front window at all the casinos and hotels along the strip, it was a good view.

I turned to Buck and said, "Welcome to the new office of Richards Investigations."

"And Security." Buck added.

**

Chapter 7

Deacon said he had to go save Lynn from Captain Weber's weekly meetings, he said good-bye to Larry and left. Buck and I went with Larry to fill out a few papers for the lease and paid him the rent. He gave me the keys and welcomed us to the neighborhood.

Buck and I went back to the office and checked it out more thoroughly this time. When a client entered the building they would find that there was a counter to the left and behind that sat a nice metal desk and chair, next to a row of low filing cabinets. To the right of the door was a small waiting area, with two genuine Naugahyde Danish modern couches flanking a low table for magazines. Off the side were two bookcases, now empty, but I had enough books to fill it. There were three hanging plant ropes, also empty, but Penny would have those filled as soon as she saw the place. Maybe one of those tree things in the corner, I'd leave the decorating to Penny. There were windows all across the front of the building so the lighting in the place was ample.

We walked down a long hallway going to the rear of the building. Up front on the left was a nice office, no windows, but with a skylight which brought in the ever present sunlight. I claimed it for myself. Across the hall from that room was another office, Buck called dibs on it for himself and his guard service, I agreed. We found two more larger rooms that were empty, but could serve as storage or conference rooms, we could do whatever we wanted with them, but we'd figure that out later. Larry came back into the building as we arrived at the back door.

"I just wanted to see if you had moved in yet." He grinned at his joke. "Now that door leads out to the back secure parking area for the whole building." I opened the door and we went out. The parking lot was large and had an eight foot tall fence topped with barbed wire going all around the lot. At the back, off a small service road was a gate, now opened with a small guard shack next to the opening.

"Do you have a guard posted at the gate?" I asked Larry.

"We had one but he quit last week, said it was too boring back here. He wasn't much of a guard, just some guy who needed a job. I guess he didn't need it that badly."

I looked to Buck and said we may be able to help him with that. I explained what we were setting up here and he smiled, saying that it was an asset to the neighborhood, a P.I. and guards running around, he liked that.

"Yeah, the travel agency and the floral store will be good neighbors too, for you I mean." He grinned. I looked around the lot, there were about a dozen cars parked, probably the employees of the other businesses in the strip mall.

We went back into the lobby as my cell phone rang, it was Penny. I went off to the side of the room to answer. "Hi babe, I'm official now, got my license and an office all since you've been gone."

"Am I gonna have to decorate this office too?" She asked knowing the answer.

"It wouldn't hurt, could use a woman's touch."

"You have your P.I. license now, so we can really get to investigating Lacey's case?" She asked.

"Yep, but I have to get a business license and my gun registered so I'm going to be busy for the rest of the afternoon. The two of you can lounge around the pool while I work." I said.

"What makes you think we aren't already in the pool?" She said then I heard a splashing sound.

"I swear you're going to turn into a porpoise if you spend all your time in the pool."

"That's all right; I'll see you when you get home. I'll be the happy porpoise floating near the surface." She laughed and disconnected.

I turned to Buck and Larry, talking about the building's past tenants and told Buck I had to go get the business license and asked if he wanted to come. He followed me out the door and Larry went back to his office. We drove up to the county building again and into the clerk's office where I filled out the paperwork for the permit and then we drove down to the police precinct to find Lynn and Deacon. Buck said he was going to stay out in the car and wait for me. The desk sergeant remembered me from the last time I was in Vegas and waved me through. I had my 9mm Glock in its case and took it with me to Lynn's office.

"Hey P.I. how's it going?" Lynn yelled as I got in her door. Deacon had seen me coming down the hall and snuck up behind me and blew in my ear. I jumped and almost clobbered him with the gun case. He smiled and I told him I brought my Glock in to be registered. Lynn came around her desk and the three of us went to take care of it.

As we walked down the hallway, Captain Weber stepped out of an office and saw me. "Damn, Richards, are you back in town? I hope

Trapper isn't with you." He chuckled remembering when Trapper and Becker pulled all their little pranks while we were out here back when Penny and I got married. Weber was a strange man, all business, but he had a good side also.

"Nope, Trapper is still back in Michigan, but Penny and I have moved here, so be ready for more serial killers." I joked. He gave me a stare and said, "I don't think we can handle that, so you are on your own. Every time you get involved in a case here, it cost us money. Well, good to see you again and we'll talk." He skittered off down the hall.

"He hasn't changed." I observed. We went to get my weapon registered and I clipped its holster to my belt and put the gun in. I now felt complete.

"Where is this cop who was primary on Lacey's investigation?" I asked.

Lynn said, "He's up in North Vegas PD precinct. Which is lucky since Deacon has to go there to take some paperwork, don't you bunny bear?"

"Stop that, if anyone hears that I'll never live it down. Sometimes you can be mean." He said quietly, she kissed him on the cheek and said to get moving.

Deacon turned to me and said, "Yeah, let's get out of here now, before I do something I may regret later." As we walked away Lynn called "In your dreams bunny bear."

Deacon slipped out the exit door quickly before any of the other cops knew the identity of bunny bear.

"She having her monthly visit?" I asked cautiously.

Deacon laughed and said, "She's a little pissed at me today about not making her coffee this morning. I insisted that she make it once in a while."

"Ok, that's grounds for divorce, even though you two aren't married yet."

"Where are you parked?" He asked.

I said in the front and Buck was in the car. I said to hold on and pulled out my cell phone. I called Buck and asked him to take my car back to the house, I'd meet him later. Buck knew where I hid the spare key to the Crown Vic and I trusted him to drive it. Besides if he wrecked it, I get to take a sledge hammer to his T-Bird.

Deacon grabbed an unmarked car out of the motor pool and we drove out Tropicana Avenue and up the strip. All the traffic heading north suddenly started driving at the speed limit, I observed.

"Yep, an unmarked cop car has that effect on traffic." Deacon laughed.

We crept along till traffic finally cleared around Charleston Avenue, so Deacon got a little heavy on the accelerator and we whizzed into the North Vegas PD parking lot shortly after.

We went into the back entrance by the police parking and Deacon took me to an office where there was an older, heavy set woman sitting at a desk surrounded by folders in varying piles. "Hey Jane, here's the files you requested from Lynn."

The woman gave him a big toothy grin and said, "Lynn just called and said you were on the way, along with the famous P.I. who saved matrimonial bliss from the Bridezilla killer."

Deacon introduced me to the woman, Jane Meerblad; she was an assistant DA and was at the North Vegas precinct to gather some info for a big case coming up. I smiled to her as she shook my hand.

She went on talking while she rummaged through the file Deacon had handed to her, "I remember when you were chasing down the killer, caused a bit of damage in the suburbs." She laughed and I knew now what Captain Weber meant when he said I cost the city money, but I was just part of the police chase, I didn't start it.

Deacon asked if there was anything else she needed from us, and she said no. He gave her a thumbs up and wished her well on her trial, then we went down the hallway to a room marked Homicide. We entered the door and I could smell coffee brewing, the life blood of the morning people.

"Don Mason should be here, I called ahead to make sure." Deacon said as we went through the maze of cubicles for what the detectives called offices. We came to one and there was an older, balding man sitting with his feet up on the desk, half asleep. Deacon whacked his feet and the man jumped.

"Crap, don't do that, I thought you were the Captain." He stood and was about a head shorter than I was. Deacon grinned and introduced us. Happily he didn't say anything about the Bridezilla killings; I was going to have to live that down.

"Lacey Lee, I remember her," he said as I asked him if he recalled her name. "Yeah, she was a psycho who dreamed up a killing to implicate some John giving her a hard time. We never found the guy; we assumed it was all made up."

"Well, I have to believe the girl was telling the truth, at least I believe her story. I wouldn't keep trying to commit suicide if it was just a scam."

Mason just gave me a dirty look, "Well, Mr. big shot P.I. that's your opinion."

60

**

Chapter 8

"I'm not challenging your take on it, Detective; I'm just going to look into it a little further. I value your opinion and would like to hear what you found during the investigation. I don't want to step on anyone's toes." I offered when I realized he was getting defensive.

He made a face that told me nothing, the guy must be good at poker. He sat back down and opened a folder on his desk. "When Detective DeAngelo called, he said you two were interested in the case so I pulled the file. Not much really to tell, she called in to 911 and said she had murdered someone, but by the time I got there she was just sitting in the room, no body, no blood, no crime. CSI checked the bathroom, found no blood anywhere and did a check on the girl's person. They found nothing, but the girl said she had cleaned up. If she had cleaned up there would have been trace in the bathroom. As I said they found none. We did a door to door search of the motel and found nothing, but a number of annoyed people. We did go to the parking lot where she said she picked up the guy who changed her tire. Now we did find a sucker stick with tranquilizer residue backing her story of being drugged. She came up negative on the rape test kit and there was not much else to go on. My team had caseloads up the ass that week and it wasn't high in my wish list to follow up. Sorry, but that's all I can give you." He went quiet and closed the file, then handed it to me. "Here take it and just get it back to me when you're done with it."

"Thanks, I appreciate your candor. I realize it's hard to chase a case without a crime. I'll keep you informed of my progress, maybe I can stir up something she may have missed." I offered to get him on my side. We thanked him and were just leaving when he said, "Hey, I gotta say you did good with the bride killer. My people were in on the end of it, thanks."

I nodded and we left. We got out to the car before saying anything. I spoke first after getting in, "That didn't tell me much more than Lynn already told me." I said as I opened the file.

"Well, there wasn't much to tell, it all was a mystery plain and simple."

"Yep, the kind I like." I smiled as Deacon put the unmarked car into gear and we sped out of the parking lot. Traffic wasn't much better around the car heading south as it was going north. We finally got to Tropicana and over to the precinct and into Lynn's office. She smiled and asked bunny bear if he delivered the file.

"If this doesn't stop right here, I'm gonna tell everyone you wear granny undies." He stood firm.

"All right, I'm done. So how was your visit with dickhead?" she asked referring to Detective Don Mason.

I replied, "Nothing more than you told me, this will be a puzzle. I hope once I get Lacey back to the scene of the crime we may come up with something."

"You're on your own now, I have a couple of gang related shootings to investigate and I need bunny ... sorry, Deacon to go along to protect me, that's all he's good for."

"Oh yeah, now I'm the gang slayer." He grinned and I said I was leaving before they started yelling.

They were going back and forth as I left, going out the front entrance to the public parking, when I realized I didn't have a car. I stood in the parking lot just as Buck drove up and smiled at me. "Did you stay here waiting for me?" I asked.

"Nope, I tailed you guys, just to see if I could do it in such a big car. You two were easy to follow." He laughed.

Sin City Murders

"Well, I'm glad you did." I said as he got out of the car and I slid behind the wheel. He settled in the passenger seat and I drove out of the parking lot for the long journey to my new home. We arrived and Buck said he had to go pick up Maria at the house and take her to get some food at Sonic's. I sort of envied him getting those good burgers and onion rings. He went to his T-Bird and drove off as I stood looking at the front of the house. It was modern with a touch of ranch to it. It was a tri-level house with a half level for a second floor that had the bedrooms in it, a short walk up a few stairs so as not to give me a heart attack climbing steps. This second level had two complete bathrooms so Penny and I could get ready in the morning without climbing over each other. The lower level was considered a rumpus room, or as I told Penny since the previous owner was a producer of a burlesque show, they probably had orgies down there. We were going to set it up as a rec-room and put a pool table, some arcade games and a couple pinball machines down there, but it wasn't high on the list of to-do's for now.

I went to the front door as Penny flung it open and I could hear the drive alarm droning on. Penny yelled that she couldn't get it to stop, so I went to the panel in the kitchen and shut it off. I showed her the proper procedure to kill the thing and she gave me a kiss on the cheek saying I was a good little security expert. I could see Lacey sitting out by the pool and Penny was still in her swimsuit.

"Is this the standard clothing to wear now?" I asked.

"It is for now but when we are alone, clothing is optional." She gave me a big tonsil search and went off to the pool again. I followed her out and sat next to Lacey and Willy while Penny took another dive into the water.

"How are you feeling now?" I asked.

"Much better now, and thank you so much for wanting to help me, it's kind of you." She replied with her cute little voice.

"Tomorrow we're going to go to my new office to get it set up. Are you okay with holding off a day or two before we started investigating?"

"Sure, I think maybe a day or two would be good, so I can get my body back in shape. May I help with getting your office set up?"

"I think Penny would like that, she'll be doing a little shopping for decorations for the office." I smiled remembering how she had such a good time decorating my office back in Michigan. I had taken the blow-up picture of her in the bikini that I put up on my office door back in Michigan and was going to hang it in my office here.

"What about your job at the casino?" I asked.

"My Uncle has put me in for medical leave to hold my job, but no pay. He looks out for me like a father." She answered. "I hope I don't lose my job, it's not the greatest but it helps to pay the bills."

I still had a great deal of money in my bank account from past cases and from my book sales of the Classmate Murders, so I asked, "How would you like to work for me while you're recuperating? I'll pay you a small salary, for things you need to get by. You'd be considered as office help."

She looked a bit stunned and I could see she was going to get teary eyed, "I would love that, thank you so much."

Penny was hanging on to the side of the pool, listening to me talk, then she said, "Yes, but he will make you work hard for the money. He's a mean boss. I work my ass off for no pay, just crumbs of food when he thinks about feeding me."

"Speaking of feeding, get dressed and I'll take everyone to Sonic's for burgers and onion rings." I said thinking about Buck going there. Penny loved that idea and jumped out of the pool and took Lacey so they could get dressed.

Willy and I sat on the plastic lawn chairs just staring at each other; I told him he could go with us also. He started his shiver and this time he let out a hearty yip, and gave me a tail wagging.

We finished eating our food, delivered by waitresses on roller skates, and it was still early in the evening so I drove us over to the new office. The lights of the strip were just coming on full force as we drove along Industrial Road, making it appear like a circus was on the edge of town. We got into the front parking lot and I was surprised to see the lights on in the office. I told the women to stay with the car, while I checked to see what was going on. I went to the door and quietly put the key in and opened the door; I had my hand on my Glock as I entered the front of the building. I could hear loud noises coming from the offices in the back and I drew my Glock now. I quietly came down the hallway as the door to the back room opened and I could see the front end of a cabinet being moved out. I thought that we were being robbed, but we had none of our own things in yet, just the office equipment that was already there. I wasn't about to lose anything that we could use so I moved close to the edge of the door and brought up my gun just as a man came out looking down the barrel my gun.

It was Buck.

**

Chapter 9

"What the hell?" was Buck's reaction until he saw me on the other end of the gun. "Jimmy, what are you doing here?"

"I brought Penny and Lacey here to show them the office; I guess you decided to start getting your office ready?" I laughed. "Hold on while I get the women." I was coming down the hall when Maria popped out of the office, she looked startled and then realized it was me. We said our hellos and I went out to the car.

Penny and Lacey were looking around as I gave the tour; Buck was busy getting his office set up. He and Maria had come back after they ate and started to work on it. Penny was eyeing the lobby area and was whispering something to Lacey. I was worried.

"I need the car keys; I'm taking Lacey with me to get some decor for this place." She said.

"Do you know where to go? Do you know where the nearest Wal-Mart is?" I asked.

She stood there for a minute thinking and then said no. Maria said she would take them in her pickup since she needed a few things too. I couldn't argue with her, she knew the town even better than I did. The three women went to the back door and out to her truck. Buck and I took a break and sat on the couches in the lobby. Willy was looking lost in the big building and he finally came over to me and wanted to be picked up, I did.

"I guess we're going to be here a while," I said. Buck smiled and went to the back room and brought out a television set he had brought in earlier and set it up in the lobby on the table in the corner. There was a cable for the TV behind the table and Buck hooked it up and turned it on. We had a picture.

"How do we have cable already?" I asked.

"When I got here, Larry was still around and said he had cable for all the offices, it was a package deal." Buck answered.

"I don't know Larry all that well, but I have a suspicion that he may have illegally tapped into the cable. We'll wait and see what happens." I said as we flipped through the channels. Buck said he brought the television out from Michigan but had no place to put it in Maria's house, so it works here.

About an hour later, the girls came back, Buck and I were volunteered to unload the stuff they bought. I brought in two big hanging plants, imitation of course, and placed them with Penny's help into the hanging ropes. A half hour later we had the front all decorated up nicely and ready for business.

"Are you going to start advertising in the papers?" Buck asked.

"That's the start, then maybe those little billboards on the bus benches. With a picture of you and me looking tough." I laughed. It was now about ten in the evening and my cell phone rang. It was Deacon.

"What's up, bunny bear?" I asked, and didn't hear anything for a second or two.

"I'm really going to ignore that. Now, I called to see what you were up to?" He growled.

"We're in the new office getting it decorated and ready for the hundreds of clients that will come streaming in soon." I smiled.

"I hope you can handle all those people. I got some good news and some not-so-good news. We've identified the guy who drugged Lacey at the parts store parking lot, that's the good news. The not-so-good news is he got away from us."

"I presume they're looking for him and how did you find him?"

"Well, Vice had a sting set up for catching johns and one of the undercover females finished her shift and was leaving the Flamingo Hotel and heading south on the Boulevard, when her car tire started to go flat.

She pulled in the parking lot by Frye's Electronic store and then a big SUV pulled in behind her. Luckily she remembered the M.O. and called for back-up. She stalled up to the part where he offered her the sucker and she badged him, pulling her gun. The back-up was just getting there but the guy managed to run around the car and disappeared into the parking lot. They got a BOLO out for him with the police woman's description and they pulled out Lacey's sketch and posted it on the LEIN. SUV was registered to one Paul Martinez and we have cars at his house now. If he goes in the wind, at least he does it without a car or his personal things."

"Well that's a step in the right direction. Sounds like this guy does this regularly, he had it planned out. Maybe grabbing women for prostitution or slavery. Lacey may have been lucky that she got away from him, but why the murder? I'm wondering if Lacey may have done it in self-defense and blanked out on the killing. Hopefully if we take her back it may jog her memory."

"Whatever, we now know that part of her story was true. Maybe the rest will be found to be true also. Hope you can find out. Well, gotta go, I'm taking Lynn to the scene of another gang shooting; it's getting bad with these guys. Nothing to worry about, it's just internal fighting within the gang. We're keeping it contained and not spilling out to the general public. Fine way to spend a night, eh?"

"Hey, how did Martinez cause the flat tires?" I asked.

"CSI said the tire was shot out. Probably Martinez used a silencer and shot the tire from the rear of her car. That's the best we can come up with for now. Gotta go, take care."

"Have a good time and I'll talk later." He disconnected and I called everyone out to the main room. After everyone was sitting in the waiting area, I told them what Deacon had related to me. Lacey looked relieved that they now knew she wasn't making it up. I said that we would start investigating her case tomorrow, but we needed to get some rest now."

I asked Buck if they were staying, he looked to Maria and said they were done. I said to lock up and took the women to the Crown Vic and headed back to the house. We pulled in and Penny said she was taking a midnight swim and asked Lacey if she wanted to join her, Lacey was all for it. They got out of the car and I pulled into the garage. It was nice now having a garage for all our cars, even the limo was just able to fit in with the door closed. We now had a three car garage and all three cars were safely out of the harsh sun of the day.

Bob Moats

I went in and Penny had disabled the alarms and they were just heading out to the pool. The temperature had dipped a bit, it was now around sixty but still warm enough for the swim, especially since the water heater was turned on. When summer arrived I probably would indulge more in the pool, which would make Penny happy. Besides, midnight skinny dipping sounded nice.

I went into my home office followed by Willy who had enjoyed the Sonic burgers as much as I did. I fired up the laptop and sat writing more about the Dominatrix Murders, since I had finished with the Vegas Showgirl Murders and my publisher was debating if they were going to take on the book. I didn't care, I had enough money to start my own publishing business and cut out the money grabbing middlemen.

I looked out my window and watched Penny swimming around in the pool. She looked so beautiful and graceful in the water. I was amazed she was still with me, thinking back to that first day we rediscovered each other during the classmate murders. Forty years of not knowing she had a serious crush on me back in high school and she wasn't disappointed when we met again. Forty wasted years but we were making up for it now.

My cell phone went off and I saw it was Deacon again, I answered but this time I wasn't going to call him bunny bear. "Hello." I said simply.

"Well, they found the sucker guy, he's dead."

"Did the cops shoot him?"

"Nope, they got a call that there was gun fire at a motel up off the strip and patrol rolled in to find him in a room dead on the floor. He had his wallet which identified him as Martinez. He was shot execution style, one to the back of the head while he was on his knees. CSI didn't get much to go on, but they still have some testing to do. We won't get much from him."

"Was it the same motel that Lacey woke in?"

"No, this one was down the road a ways from where she was."

"This is sounding like there's much more to it than just random grabbing of women. There's someone else involved, maybe his partner's angry that he almost got caught, this could be dangerous for Lacey, since she got away from them."

Deacon was silent for a moment, "True, but they've had a good amount of time to go after her since that day she called us in. Although, nothing was mentioned in the media about her involvement because there was no provable crime. Maybe they figured she doesn't know who they are, she may be safe."

"I hope so, with the murder of Martinez this could go bad since he was the one to grab her, they must know her. I'll have to be extra careful now. Thanks for the heads up on it," I said and we finished the call.

I sat back in my chair looking out the window at the women frolicking in the pool. So happy and so unaware of what could be brewing. I decided to wait till morning to tell them of this latest news, no sense in spoiling their evening. I went back to working on my story.

**

Chapter 10

The fat man sat back in his office chair glaring at the man standing before his desk. "What the hell were you two thinking, Mosh? Did you have to kill him in the motel? Why didn't you just drive him out to the desert and kill him?" He went silent waiting for Mosh to answer.

"He was making trouble for us. Willis was barely able to get him down on the floor to do him; he wasn't going to go quietly out to the desert. After Willis fired the gun I heard people yelling, so we panicked and ran. I'm sorry boss, but Martinez would have been picked up by the cops eventually and the weasel he was, he would have ratted us all out."

"Fine, now he's dead so he can't rat anyone. What about the girl? Has she gotten back her memory?"

"I talked to a few of my people inside the hospital and they said that she was released into the custody of some P.I. from Michigan. I don't know what it's about, but I was told she still doesn't remember anything."

"Well, keep an eye on her, if she even gets a flicker of remembrance, do what you have to do. The bitch almost ruined the whole set-up by disappearing before we could implicate her. It was better that we had let her live so the cops think she's just some whack job. Too bad she's lousy at killing herself; we may have to help her try it again. Now go take care of business and get outta my sight."

The fat man sat back again as Mosh went out. He picked up his phone and buzzed his secretary saying, "Get Mason on the phone."

~~*~~

Bob Moats

I was up early, looking out to the backyard; I saw Penny and Lacey doing the porpoise thing in the pool. This was going to be a daily affair now, I guess. I went to the kitchen and made two pieces of toast, I felt hungry this morning, and then I watched from the dining room as the girls played. Willy was still inside at the patio door watching out; I guess he must have hid when Penny said they were going out to the pool. He's no dummy. I finished my toast giving Willy a portion when he saw me eating; I stood and went out the glass door followed by the dog. I stopped to feed the goldfish under the ugly statue still pouring water and went to sit on the plastic chairs by the pool.

Penny saw me and swam over splashing me a little with her hand. "Stop it, I don't need this." I complained.

"Wussy, a little water won't hurt you. So what's on the agenda this morning?"

"I thought we'd run by the office first to organize and then head to the motel where Lacey ended up." I said this as Lacey swam down the long pool towards us.

"Good morning Mr. Richards."

"No, call me Jim. I'm not an old man."

Penny smiled and said under her breath, "Like hell you're not."

"I heard that."

"Sorry Sweetie, you're as young as you feel."

I asked them to get out of the pool; I had something to tell them. They both came up the steps and grabbed towels to dry. They then pulled chairs up to sit by me.

"Deacon called me late last night to say they found the sucker man dead in a motel up off the north end of the strip. He was identified and he was killed execution style, so there has to be a bigger picture here for this to happen. I'm concerned for Lacey's safety now, so we have to be alert."

Penny's mouth tightened and said, "I need to get a gun."

I looked to her and thought a moment. "That's actually not a bad idea. I'll call Lynn and see what we can arrange. Have you ever fired a gun?"

"You mean other than when I shot your enemy Nick North? Yes, I used to go hunting with my father. He was a big supporter of the NRA, card carrying gun nut he was. I was shooting at targets since I was fourteen, he insisted on it."

"You have so many mysteries about you, why haven't you told me about this before?" I asked.

"Why didn't you tell me your little secret that you could swim before this," she mimicked.

"Okay, we have some serious talking to do about our little secrets. Anyway, we can get you set-up with a weapon, I'd feel safer." I looked to Lacey, "We're going to have to take you back to the scene of the crime to see if we can jog your memory, that won't be a problem for you?"

"No, the faster I get these nightmares out of my head the better. I actually slept well last night; I think it helped because I was here."

"Tell me about the nightmares, describe them." I asked.

"They're always the same, I'm in the room of the motel and there are two men dragging a body towards the bed where I was lying. I was groggy, I think I was waking from the drugs the sucker man gave me, but I was pretending to be asleep. The two men put the dead guy in the bed next to me and then they started to stab him with the knife, many times. I felt one man reach over and put the knife in my hand and they walked out. I looked over to the body and that's when I would wake up every time from the nightmare."

"Actually it sounds like you may be describing what may have really happened that night. You've only seen this in dreams, no memory about it?"

"No, just the dreams, over and over again. Maybe I'm trying to remember and my mind is playing it all over again."

"Well, we still have to find out why you woke in the room with no crime scene."

"If we are going to start our day, we need to get dressed," Penny said to Lacey. They got up and went off into the house leaving Willy and me alone with our thoughts. I had no idea as to Lacey's condition, but hopefully we could go through the steps at the motel to get her memory working.

I got up and went inside to get my equipment to go with me, my Palm TX, pocket knife, cell phone and my Glock in its holster. I was ready for most anything. I thought about getting Penny a gun, I'd have to call Lynn to see if we could get her a CCW. I took my cell phone out and dialed her number, she answered after two rings, must not have been busy.

"Hey Fearless Fosdick, how are you today." I laughed at her reference from back when we kidded about the characters from the old Dick Tracy comic strip.

"I'm fine Tracy, I need a favor. I want to get Penny a small gun to carry for protection; God knows she needs it the way she gets kidnapped. Can you start the wheels going for a CCW?"

"Sure, go over to Flamingo and Pecos, there's a small gun shop there and the owner knows me well so he won't cheat you. Drop my name and pick out a suitable gun for her, then she'll have to sign up for the classes and fire the thing so she can get the permit. He can get her pushed through the classes and we'll get the gun permit and CCW all taken care of at one time. Has she fired a weapon before?"

I told her about Penny's father and she laughed. "Good you two don't have many secrets."

"Yeah, I'm a little frightened of her right now. But I'll get everything taken care of and keep you informed, thanks." We finished up and Penny came out of the bedroom dressed like she was going on a safari, khaki shorts, khaki military shirt, and hiking boots. All she was missing was the Pith helmet. "Where'd you get that outfit?"

"I had to dress like a big game hunter on one of my shows when we had an animal handler so I got this outfit." she smiled and kissed me.

I looked past her out the huge picture window and saw Lacey coming around the front to the door. Then I saw a car drive by a little too slowly and the driver was watching

Lacey. I went to the door quickly, out to the porch, then walked down the driveway quickly towards the car. The driver saw me and sped away. I got to the road in time to see his plate number and wrote it down on my Palm PDA notepad to give to Lynn. Penny was on the porch with Lacey asking me what was wrong.

"Probably nothing, some pervert watching Lacey but I got his plates, so we'll see." I walked to the garage and keyed in the code on the pad to open the overhead door to the Crown Vic's berth. I went in and drove the car out letting the women and Willy get in.

We pulled out the drive and were heading down the road, I was watching my rearview mirror for the car to come around, but didn't see him until I got more into the city where traffic was making it easier to tail me. He was about five cars back but it was him. I pulled my cell and put it on speaker after dialing Lynn.

"Sorry to bother you again, but I got a tail."

"Animal or human?" She asked with a laugh.

**

Chapter 11

"Not sure, but I got his plate number, want it?"

"Shoot." I gave it to her and I could hear her typing something. "The LEIN says it's a stolen car. Where are you now?"

"I'm on Sahara just coming up to Buffalo Drive, what do you want me to do?"

"Stay on Sahara and try to get stopped at each light while I call for a couple of patrol cars. Keep the phone open. I got the make of the car, a Ford Escort, is that correct?"

"I don't know one car from another."

Lacey said from the back seat that it was, she had heard the conversation and looked back to see the car. I thanked her and Lynn had heard her through the phone. She made the call, I presumed I was in her car so I just snailed it on down the road. I watched for the patrol cars to come screaming by us, as I drove on slowly making a few people mad around me. I saw a number of middle fingers. She asked through the phone what was going on, I said nothing at the moment. Then I saw the patrol cars in my mirror as they came up behind my stalker. The driver must have seen them also as he quickly turned right, speeding down

Decatur Boulevard being pursued by the cops. I kept on going and decided to go get Penny her gun, we may need it. I told Lynn what we were doing and where the pursuit was going, she thanked me and we disconnected.

I turned right on South Valley View Boulevard and down to Flamingo, then heading east out past the strip and finally arriving at Pecos pulling into the plaza where the gun shop was. Penny got all bouncy and asked if we were getting her a gun, I had to chuckle watching her get excited. We went in and found the owner, Bert Randle, and I dropped Lynn's name. He smiled taking us to the side where he had all his hand guns in a display case after I told him what we needed.

"This here is a nice little number; it will fit in a purse and is light enough for the little lady."

"Hell with small and light, I want firing power. Let me see that Smith and Wesson .38." I was trying not to laugh as he looked surprised and brought out the gun. Penny spun the cylinder, looked down the sights and asked if she could fire it. Lacey, carrying Willy, was a little surprised that they had a firing range in the back. Bert set up a target for her and gave us ear protectors. Penny took stance and fired off a number of rounds in quick succession hitting the target in a nice tight two inch hole. I was shocked, so was Bert.

"Well I guess you've had lessons," he spoke happily. "Shall I wrap it or you going to pack?"

I laughed and said, "She's not licensed to carry yet. Lynn said you'd get her into class and get her through the process."

He looked around and said quietly, "I can fluff the classes and get her registered sooner."

"What's this going to cost us?" I asked.

"Hey, you're friends of Lynn's, so nothing, but just put in a good word." He gave me a toothy smile and I said it was fine with me. He took the target and signed it as her firing test, took us up front and pulled out the paperwork and did a bit of writing. He stamped it and said to take it to Lynn and she'd process it from there. I wondered if this was legal and he said it wasn't the first time this was done. "Hey, it's Vegas baby, lots of things happen here and stay here. That's why Lynn sent you to me." He gave me the toothy smile again and I thanked him, then paid him for the gun and his time.

We went out to the car and drove down to Tropicana and over to Lynn's precinct. We took the gun in and found Lynn. She welcomed Lacey and had us come into her office. She said, "The officers pursued your tail until he pulled into a shopping plaza, jumped from the car and disappeared, but we got CSI dusting the car for prints, maybe they'll get lucky, if he didn't wear gloves. I'll let you know what we find. Now you went to see my buddy Bert, what happened?"

I handed the paperwork to Lynn.

"Bert said you condone this?" I asked her.

She gave me a grin and said to keep our mouths shut and go with the flow. Penny said it was fine with her, I agreed. Lynn took down the serial number and processed the form we gave her. She looked at the target and gave Penny a stare, "You actually shot this?"

"Yep, with my eyes closed." She replied.

"I hope you stay on our side. So you can carry now. Just don't shoot the wrong people, too much paperwork. I have a question," she asked looking at the target Penny aced, "when you shot at Nick North back when you were out here for the convention, you could have taken him out, right?"

"I didn't want to kill him; I just wanted him to suffer in jail, that's why I shot him in the gun arm." She gave me her evil little smile.

"Okay, that's good to know. Let's see the gun." Penny took it out of the case and handed it to Lynn. "Nice piece, good choice. Now make good use of it. So where are you guys heading now?"

"I thought we would go to the motel to start Lacey's therapy for recovery." I smiled. "I hope we aren't going to be followed again."

"Well, keep me on your speed dial, and keep me informed as to anything you can find." We thanked her and went out. Deacon was coming down the hallway with another cop hauling a handcuffed gangbanger to interrogation. He waved and went into the room.

We got to the car and Willy was bouncing all over, probably cussing us out for leaving him alone. He jumped on Lacey in the back seat and curled up. I looked to Penny and said, "Looks like our baby is deserting us."

We drove up to the motel using the address that was in the file I still had from Detective Mason. We pulled in and went to the office finding a young woman behind the counter.

"Hi, my name is Jim Richards and this is..." She started screaming, "Oh My God, you're the woman from that TV show aren't you?" She was bouncing up and down like Penny was one of the Back Street Boys.

Penny went to her and took her hands to settle her. "Yes I am, now we need your help. Do you think you can take a breath and do that?"

She was wide-eyed and nodded her head vigorously. "Yes, I can, what do you need? Anything."

I had consulted the file and found out the room number. I asked if there was anyone in that room at the moment. She looked at the registry and said it was unoccupied and I asked if we could see it. I showed her my temporary P.I. ID and introduced her to Lacey.

"Oh wow, I remember you, I was here the day the cops all came swooping in and checked all the rooms. They found nothing though if I remember." she bubbled.

"Right, good memory, but now I'd like to find out who was registered in that room the night it happened." I asked.

"I can tell you now, there was no one registered in that room, which I thought was strange that she was in that room."

"So you're saying she was in the room and no one was supposed to be in there?"

"Yeah, that's the deal."

"Can we look in the room, is that permitted?"

"Well, no one is in there so I guess you don't need a warrant or anything." She smiled and grabbed the key, yelling into a door behind her that she was going out. A younger man came out looking like he hadn't slept well or was drugged up. The girl, who told us her name was Sissy, took us to the room and opened it up. I went in followed by Lacey, then Sissy, Penny held back watching the parking lot. I smiled at my little P.I. and thought I would have to get her bonded and licensed too. This may be a new career for her.

I looked around the room and asked Lacey to sit on the bed and think back to the day it happened. She stared at the room for a good two minutes; I wasn't going to rush her. She started to look sad, I said to try and remember that we are here with her.

"Think about your dream, does this room look like the room in your dream?"

She was still silent and then quietly said no, it wasn't. I asked her to close her eyes and describe the room from her dream.

"It was done in a darker color, dark green walls, and really bad pictures on the wall. The type you'd buy at a yard sale. The bed spread was red and smelled musty. There was a lamp on the table; it was the only light in the room. The carpet was a rust color and dirty. That's all I can see." She opened her eyes and looked at the room. "This isn't the room."

Sissy was standing next to me and said, "That room she described sounds like the Wayfarer Motel, they have rooms like that."

I asked, "Where is the Wayfarer Motel?"

Sin City Murders

She pointed out the front window at a motel across the street. The sign said Wayfarer Motel. I thanked her and asked Lacey to follow. We went back to the car and I gave Sissy a tip and thanked her again. She looked at the twenty and gave me a big grin, then she yelled to wait. She ran into the office and came out with a pad of paper and pen. She asked Penny for her autograph and Penny signed the thing. Sissy thanked her and went back to the office.

I drove across the road and into the Wayfarer parking lot. We got out and went to the office, this time there was an old woman with grey hair and thick glasses standing behind the counter. I introduced myself and asked if she remembers a murder that was supposed to have been committed across the street. She stared at me and said, "You got the wrong motel mister, a murder happened here, not across the street. I know because I called the cops that night I found the bodies. Two people, a man and woman, both dead by stab wounds. The cops said the woman stabbed the guy and committed suicide."

I looked at Penny and asked the woman, "Did this happen on February 10th of this year?"

"Close, I found the bodies on February 11th, but the cops said they were killed a day earlier, so it may have been on the 10th."

I took out my cell phone to call Lynn, saying, "We got a new mystery."

**

Chapter 12

Lynn came flying into the Wayfarer parking lot as we stood outside waiting. She exited her car and came up saying she called Mason about the murder but was told he took a few personal days off. She couldn't find anyone who remembered the crime there, but she put in a call to a friend in CSI to get anything they had on the case. She went into talk to the desk lady and we stood behind her as she asked questions. I was watching Lacey as she was starting to look upset.

"Lacey you seem to be bothered by something, what is it?"

"It's the smell here; I'm sure it's the same I remember now from the room."

Lynn heard Lacey and asked the woman if we could get in the room where the murder happened. The woman checked the register and said it was vacant, so she got the key and took us to the room. We went in and suddenly Lacey went crazy; crying and panicking. Penny grabbed her and held tight. I came to her and asked her what was wrong.

"This is the room; I know it is, from my dream. Oh, God, get me out of here please!" She cried. Penny took her out and I looked to Lynn.

"What's going on? A crime of murder in this motel, and a report of the same type of crime across the street a day apart, but no one thought to associate the two?" I asked.

"It's not my jurisdiction, I don't know why. But when I find Mason, I'll be sure to ask. I think Lacey was part of this but somehow got away and ended up across the street. How I don't know." Her cell phone rang and she answered. "Yeah, the Wayfarer Motel, right... who was primary investigator? Really. That says a lot. Thanks I owe you one." She disconnected and smiled to me. "I'll give you three guesses but the first two don't count."

"Mason," was all I said.

"Yep, now I really need to track him down. This stinks of collusion."

"Think this out, Lacey gets grabbed, brought to a motel where she is placed with a dead body, but she wanders off somehow and ends up in another motel across the street. She's missing so someone had to put another woman in her place. Lots of planning for what? Who was the dead guy?"

92

"Don't know until I can get hold of the case file. I'll explain this all to Captain Weber and see if he can get cooperation from North Vegas PD."

"I think Lacey needs to be really watched now, if she gets her memory back of their faces she could be in danger, if she's not already." I went to the door and looked out to the parking lot where Penny was consoling Lacey who was hugging Willy. I was getting a bad feeling from this all, cops could be involved and more than one bad guy was setting up death beds.

We thanked the lady for letting us in the room and went to our cars. Lynn said she'd do some checking and talk to Weber, she'd let me know what happens. I said we were going to the new office to reconnoiter and regroup, maybe even rest. I drove out followed by Lynn and we parted down by Tropicana as I headed to the office. As we pulled up to the front of the building, there was a line of men outside the building. I wondered what Buck was up to. I parked and Penny, Lacey still holding Willy and I went to the entrance.

"Hey the line ends back there." One of the men at the front of the line said as I tried to go in.

I looked at him and said, "What's your name?"

He gave me a hard stare and said, "Nick."

"Well, Nick this is *my* office and intend to go in whether you like it or not. Now if you're here for a job, I would suggest that you be a little more polite."

Nick smiled and opened the door for us, saying "Have a nice day, sir."

I mumbled, "Better," and we went in. The waiting area had a number of men standing or sitting and Maria was handing out papers and pencils to the men. She saw us and smiled saying Buck was in his office.

I told Penny and Lacey to sit in my office till I found out what was going on. I already figured that Buck had somehow gotten word out that he was hiring guards and these men were applying for the job. I hoped Buck could pay all the people he hired.

I entered his office and he had some guy in a chair. Buck stood and said, "Jimmy, didn't expect you back this morning. I was just interviewing a few prospects for the guard service." He looked to the man in the chair and said he was finished with him, thanked him for coming and he would be informed of his decision. The man left and I sat in the now vacant chair.

"So how did you get all these people here so fast, did you put an ad in the paper?"

"Well, I called all the Harley shops and put out the word that I was hiring for men who could take on the job of guarding. I think I need tough men to handle the criminal element." He gave me his walrus smile and sat back.

I was suppressing a laugh and said, "That works for me, but you aren't putting them on payroll until they are placed somewhere."

"Oh man, no, I'm telling them there is no pay until they are working. I'm no dummy and I don't have the funds to do something foolish like that."

"What about uniforms?"

"I talked to a uniform shop this morning and they are going to front me the outfits if I agree to do all my business with them and pay on time. I sweet talked a little old lady owner into the deal."

"Great, now you have to sweet talk to our insurance man about getting bonded. Can't do the job without bonding."

"Already did, he'll bill us next month after I get a couple places going."

"Speaking of that, have you lined up any places yet?"

"You'll love this, I got two car dealers lined up, they both are unhappy with this Retcho Guard service and have agreed to give us a try. Oh and Lacey's friend, name's Mac Knight, called me this morning, he's all for taking a position with me. I may put him in charge of the men, since he's experienced and huge. He came in after we talked on the phone and he just about filled the doorway coming in."

"I hope it goes well for you, now I'll tell you what we found out with Lacey." I proceeded to tell him of our morning and then told him about Penny getting her gun.

"Bout time you did, that poor woman has been attacked and kidnapped enough times to warrant having a gun." He laughed. "So it sounds like the cops may be in on it, eh?"

"Yeah, Lynn is going to do some digging. Just watch out for anything suspicious involving Lacey. Keep an eye on her too."

Buck agreed and I said I'd get out of the way so he could finish his interviews. I was happy for Buck, he was enjoying his new role and I hoped it went well. He seemed to be on top of everything, getting all the details done and ironed out. I went to my office and closed the door, to keep all the commotion out and sat at the desk. I didn't have all my stuff on the desk yet, that would come later. Penny and Lacey were talking as I took out the Vegas phone book that was in the desk drawer and looked up the local phone company. Since I remember the last time I lived here there were a couple of phone companies to use, so I picked the one I had used before. I got hold of customer service on my cell phone and made arrangements to have the phone lines installed, one for me, one for Buck and one for fax or computer.

About three hours later, I had my office set up and even put Penny's bikini picture on the back of my door, she liked it. The applicants had all finally gone and Buck had a pile of applications to sort through. He came into my office.

"I had a number of former guards from Retcho; they didn't have many nice things to say about them. I got a call from one of the dealerships and they want us to start this Friday night, so I got to pick a couple of men and get this all situated. My first gig. I like." He went back out and I went to the lobby counter and reception desk, finding Penny and Lacey getting it set up. They had taken the car and Lacey guided Penny to Wal-Mart again to get some office supplies and she bought a fax machine and copy machine all in one. I was proud of her for the initiative she was taking and told her so.

"So how about lunch?" I asked. They both said they'd like that and we went over to an "In-N-Out" burger outlet. I asked Buck and Maria but they weren't hungry. We brought our food back to the office and sat eating. I was looking through the phone book again for the advertising department of the Review-Journal newspaper and made a call. I was told they would send a rep out to discuss a display ad in their paper and we set a time and date. I sat back in my desk chair and watched the women talking and eating. It amazed me how they found things to talk about.

My cell phone rang and the caller ID said unknown, but I answered anyway. The voice on the phone said, "Richards, watch your back." and they hung up. Great, now I'm getting threats.

**

Chapter 13

I set the caller ID block and hit the redial callback code and waited to see if it would work. I heard the phone ring and some woman answered, "Retcho Guard Service, how may I help you?" I hung up. A threat against Buck, I corrected myself.

I went across the hall and told Buck, he wondered how they got my number and not his. I picked up one of his business cards and looked at it. The number listed was for Richards Investigations and it had my cell phone number listed, then Buck's number was printed below his name at the bottom. They called my number first which I explained to Buck.

"So they got hold of one of the cards I gave out, they must be worrying." He said with a smile.

"I hope they aren't planning on holding to their threat. I got the call recorded on my phone since my cell phone records all calls coming in. I can play it for Lynn and see what she says."

"I'll talk to Mac and see what he knows about Retcho, maybe he can tell me what to expect." Buck said as he searched for Mac's application.

"Do that, we don't need threats from rival companies. It's just not professional." I went out and found Penny and Lacey watching the TV. "I didn't authorize a break for you two."

Penny showed me her middle finger and Lacey smiled for the first time since we had gotten back from the motel. I hoped that finally seeing the room would help her get over her dreams, we would see.

It was getting late, so we packed it in and headed home. Lacey had been very quiet the entire ride to the house and Penny left her alone for now. We arrived and Penny asked Lacey if she wanted to take a swim and Lacey said she was tired and just wanted to rest, so she went off to the guesthouse.

"I hope she's going to be okay. Maybe some rest will do her some good, to get the memories out." Penny said as we came in the front door.

"At least we now know that there was a crime. Lynn said she'd dig around to find out why the North Vegas cops didn't connect the two crimes. I hope we don't have crooked cops again, I really hate when that happens, takes all the good out of police work." I went to the kitchen to check the security panel and reset the thing.

Penny sat at the snack counter admiring her new gun. I said to be careful not to shoot herself; she knew enough not to point it at me even in jest, but she did make her hand into a gun and fire at me. "I may need some extra spending money, have you kept up your life insurance policy?" she said with a smile.

I looked to her and wondered what she was getting at. "If I died you wouldn't have much to live on from my insurance." I said nonchalantly.

"Too late to hide the fact that I would be a rich widow if you croaked. Our insurance man called three month ago to see if I was interested in increasing my policy to be more in line with yours. I did manage to trick him into telling me what you're worth in death. I must say I was impressed that you thought so much of me to take care of my widowhood." She gave me a big smile and I shook my head. I couldn't keep anything from her, it was futile.

We plopped on the couch with our beer and chips and turned on the huge television, flipping through the channels till we came to a good comedy we both liked. This TV was twice as big as the one back in Michigan, so we felt like we were at the movies with the big screen. Around 11, we drifted to the bedroom and crawled into bed. Penny had her .38 on her bed stand and I had my Glock on mine. Nice to think we were protected. We both agreed that we were a bit worn from the day to indulge in any psychical activities, so we just cuddled and eventually fell asleep.

I looked at the clock on the bed stand when the property alarms went off around 5 A.M. and jumped up. I threw on a pair of pants and pulled a shirt on, grabbing my Glock and headed to the kitchen to check the monitor. Penny was just coming out behind me with her .38 as I was using the remote control to scan the cameras around the property. I felt Penny put her hand on my shoulder and pointed out to the pool, in the bare illumination of the security sensor light, we could see that Lacey was standing at the edge of the pool.

I flipped on the rest of yard lights then we went out and over to her, she just stood as though in a trance. I came up on one side of her and Penny her other. She was standing at the very edge of the pool, her eyes were glazed looking and she just stared at the water.

"Lacey?" Penny said quietly. No answer. Penny looked to me and said softly, "She's sleepwalking. I had a doctor on one of my shows who covered this." She took Lacey by the shoulders and turned her away from the pool and led her to one of the lawn chairs, getting her to sit.

"You aren't supposed to wake a sleepwalker are you?" I asked.

"That's a myth, but if you do wake one, there could be problems. A sleepwalker may panic by being surprised and take a swing at you, which is about the only bad thing that could happen." She sat next to Lacey as I stood watching them. "Lacey," Penny said to her, then called her again softly. Lacey slowly turned her head to Penny then back to the pool. She started to look like she was struggling with her thoughts and her face went contorted as she screamed and jumped up, running toward the pool and fell in.

Penny looked as shocked as I must have, we placed our guns on the ground and we both ran to the pool and dove in after her. We managed to bring her back up and over to the side. I jumped out and pulled her up while Penny was pushing at her. We laid her on the ground and Penny got a towel from a table, rolling it to place under her head.

"Looks like her nightmares haven't ended." I said.

Lacey was sputtering from the water that had gotten in her mouth and looked to us with panicked eyes. Penny held her down and called her name telling her it was us and she was safe. She finally stared at Penny and asked what she was doing out here.

We sat her up and Penny said, "You were sleepwalking, do you remember what you were dreaming?"

She was thinking and said, "Yes, I remember the two men stabbing the man next to me and then they were talking and went out of the room. I stood and went to the bathroom to wash off the blood from holding the knife and off my body. I went back out to the room and found my clothes and put them on, and then I saw the man and all the blood and had to throw up so I went back into the bathroom. I must have fallen asleep at the toilet and that's when I woke up in the wrong room." She looked to us, frightened but relieved. "I remember now, I remember their faces and one of the men told the other to call someone named Mason." I got a chill hearing that. "They thought I was still passed out from the drug and said they'd kill me just before the police got there, to look like I had killed myself." She started crying and Penny held on to her rocking her gently.

"I'll call Lynn this morning and have her come by to talk to Lacey," I said softly. We were all wet and Penny said she was taking Lacey to the guesthouse to get dry clothes and they would come back to the house. I picked up our guns, went in to change and about twenty minutes later they came in. Penny sat Lacey on the couch in the living room and went to change. I sat on an easy chair across from her and said she was going to be alright. Penny came out about five minutes later and sat next to Lacey letting her put her head on Penny's shoulder.

"I remember everything now," she said, "I know that they had planned to make it look like I had killed the man and that would take suspicion off of their people, whoever they were. I heard one of the men say the guy in bed was becoming a pain in the ass and he wasn't going to cause any more trouble." She was quiet for a few minutes, we gave her the space. "They set the whole thing up and were using me to take the fall. Bastards."

I had to chuckle to myself when she said that. Penny looked to me and smiled. "I think maybe Lacey is going to be better for now, knowing what happened, but the trauma still has to be worked out."

I looked to Lacey, she seemed to be back asleep. I got an extra pillow out of the linen closet and brought it to Penny who placed it on the couch and set Lacey down to rest on it. We both stood and watched her for a while.

"I'll stay up with her, till we can get Lynn to come by and sort this out." Penny said.

"No way I'm going to sleep now, too much excitement. I'll guard the house, you guard Lacey." I sat on the recliner and Penny sat on the easy chair. Willy came out from the bedroom looking half asleep, probably wondering what the hell everyone was doing up so early.

**

Chapter 14

Lynn and Deacon arrived around 9 A.M. and Lynn sat on the couch next to Lacey listening to her tell the same thing she told us this morning. After Lacey finished, Lynn just sat thinking silently while we all watched.

"Are you sure the men said to call someone named Mason?" Lynn asked.

"Yes, I remember the name now because it was the same name as the cop who came to check my story. I couldn't remember what had happened that night so I didn't associate the name. Could it have been the same man?" Lacey asked.

"Maybe," she answered, and then turned to us, "I talked to Weber this morning and explained the whole thing to him and he feels something is rotten in Denmark, I quote him. He tried to get hold of Mason but the guy is not responding to calls. He also talked to the Captain of North Vegas PD and then let me explain the situation. North Vegas PD Captain Sustaine said he will give us cooperation on the matter. He said we could come get the case book and talk to whoever we needed to. He also said he was putting out a few men to track down Mason." Lynn turned to Lacey and asked,

"Do you feel well enough to talk to a few more people about this?"

"Anything to get this solved. I hoped last night was to be the end of it." She said quietly.

"Good, it will help." Lynn turned to Penny and me, "Okay, just keep an eye on her till I get word to you if we find Mason and after I read over his file. As Weber says, something is rotten in Denmark." She smiled and got up.

They said their good-byes and left. Penny looked to Lacey and asked, "Feel like a quick dip in the pool, this time while you're awake." Lacey laughed and said she could use it. Her body was stiff from sleeping on the couch. They went off and I stayed in the room holding Willy and saying, "We'll just hang in here away from that nasty pool, won't we?" Willy gave me a yip and I smiled.

~~*~~

Buck had six men in the office and he was giving them details on the new job that they had coming this week. He gave them sheets of paper with the address of the uniform shop and the dealership they would be guarding. He told them to get their uniforms before they start working or they wouldn't work. Buck said he didn't tolerate screwing around and sleeping on the job, and would have Mac Knight checking on them. If I had been there I would have reminded Buck of his work ethic, but Buck was demanding better of his team.

Buck explained that two of the men would have to use their own cars to patrol the lot, but they would get a gas allowance and hopefully as business picked up, they would have company cars to use. He said he would be there at start of shift with one of the managers from the dealership to get them set up and show them what to do. He turned them loose and sat with Mac Knight in his office.

"You told me that Retcho may carry out their threat against us, what do you think they might do?" He asked Mac.

"If they are still as stupid as they were when I worked for them, they could do anything. I think our guards are going to have to be on their toes the first week in. I know that dealership because I worked it one week when a guard had to go for an operation. It's not difficult, but lots of bad corners and back areas to watch. They have security cameras and they do work, so it may help in case they try something."

"Good, thanks for that. I guess we will just have to wait till Friday to see." Buck thanked him for coming in and Mac left. Buck picked up the phone and called me to tell me about his first day as boss.

~~*~~

The fat man was red in the face as he screamed at Mosh, standing like a scared rabbit. "Idiot! Fool! You're lucky you were wearing gloves so they couldn't get a fix on you from the car. You don't have the brains to follow anyone, call Willis for that stuff, dummy. Now what have you found out from Mason?"

"He said that the P.I. is trying to help the girl to get over her nightmares about the night we whacked Brantley. He said we should do something about her."

"This is going to come apart if we don't cover ourselves. We have too much invested in this to let it fall apart. Maybe having Mason in our pocket might get us burned. Get Willis and take care of Mason, do you know where he is?"

"Yeah, he's hiding out at his girlfriend's place. Should we do a number on the two of them?"

"Whatever it takes, just don't leave any evidence." Mosh left and the fat man mumbled, "I got idiots working for me. Never hire family again."

~~*~~

Sin City Murders

I sat at pool side with Willy as the girls finally decided to get out. They were toweling off when my cell phone rang, it was Lynn. I stood and went to the kitchen for some privacy as she was explaining to me that she had the case file and there were some omissions in the report. Like the connection to Lacey's report of the same type of crime just across the street.

"I was thinking this morning, we now know Lacey sleepwalks, so when she said she fell asleep in the bathroom of the first motel, maybe she sleepwalked across the road to the other motel and somehow got into a room." I said.

"Well, it's the only good explanation I would have. Whatever, we still need to find Mason. Right now he's the link. Oh and here's the kicker, the man who was murdered in the motel was Eldridge Brantley, a city councilman. The cops were ordered to keep it quiet because he was found in a motel with a woman other than his wife. They covered up the scandal, but it was reported to the media that he had died, no other details released. I know Brantley was pushing to ban any form of prostitution in and around Vegas, which could be a reason for his death."

"So someone wanted him out of the way for his votes, what better way to do it than have him in a love nest, dead."

"Yep and he was replaced with a liberal who was all for legalizing prostitution. All sounds like a plot to me." Lynn said.

"You don't have any evidence of the people who may have been involved?"

"They've been careful enough to cover themselves; CSI came up with nothing to implicate any outsiders other than Brantley and the woman, who had priors for prostitution. Maybe after they found out Lacey slipped away, they grabbed a nearby hooker to finish it."

"Well, we'll be watching out for any attempts on Lacey now, they should be worried that she may talk. Penny is not going to like this if she knows we maybe stalked."

"Yeah, be careful she doesn't shoot you in the night now that she is armed and dangerous." Lynn laughed and said she had to go.

I disconnected the call and stood looking out the window to the girls at the pool side taking in the sun. I let them rest for another half hour, then went out to say I wanted to take them to the office. I didn't say why; that I wanted Buck to keep an eye on them for me while I did some snooping. We went to get dressed and I pulled the Crown Vic out of the garage. They came out to the car and we drove over to the office. I had called Buck from the car to be sure he was there and he said he was going to be in the office all day.

I pulled up to the building, took the women in and found Buck working happily at his desk and Mac Knight was with him.

"Hey Jimmy, I hear you're getting Lacey all squared away." He said with his big smile.

"Yep, we're getting closer to finding out what's happening." I said as Lacey came up behind me and saw Mac.

"Mac! How are you doing?" she said. Mac jumped up, went by me to her and they got into a big bear hug. She almost disappeared in his hug since he was huge against her small body. He put her down and gave her a sisterly kiss on her cheek.

"I'm good, but where have you been hiding? I've been by your place a few times but you were never there. I even stopped at the casino but your uncle told me you were off work for a while. He didn't seem to want to tell me much more. You okay?"

"I am now, since Jim and Penny have been helping me." she replied.

"Is this about the incident at the motel?" He asked.

"Yeah, come on and sit down and I'll tell you about it." They went to the waiting area, sat on the couch and talked.

I went up to Buck's desk, "I'm going to check on something at the motel, so keep an eye on Penny and Lacey while I'm gone." I had already explained to him what had happened this morning when he called earlier and he understood the situation.

I went into my office and Penny was sitting in my chair, letting Willy sprawl out on the desk. "Taking over now?" I asked.

"Nope, just seeing what it's like to be the boss," she smiled.

"Why bother, you already are the boss."

"Yes, and don't forget it," she said with her evil little smile.

**

Chapter 15

I drove up the strip until I arrived at the motel Lacey woke in that fateful morning. I parked and went to the office and found Sissy still behind the desk. "Hi Sissy. How are you today?"

"Hey, I'm good, where's your TV lady today?" she bubbled.

"She's minding the office. I've made her my secretary now that she has retired from doing her show. I just came by to ask a few more questions, do you have the time?" I said.

"Go ahead, shoot. I'm all ears."

"So you were here the morning that the girl woke in the room?"

"Yep, I was on duty when she used the room phone to call this office crying for help. I called the cops."

"Do you have any idea how she managed to get into the room if she wasn't registered?"

"Nope, it was a puzzle to me. I told the cops the same thing, she didn't belong here. The one cop in charge didn't seem too interested in her either. I thought that was strange. He was real brisk about her too."

"Your doors to the rooms are all locked when there are no guests?"

"Yep, other than when the maids clean, then they leave the doors open while they work. Hey, you think maybe she slipped in that way, while the maids were cleaning?"

"It's a possibility. Do you know who was on duty that morning?"

Sissy looked at a book on the desk and flipped some pages, then said, "Yeah, Marianna Valez was on duty that morning, but she quit shortly after that day. Don't know why, she just called in to say she quit and hung up."

114

"Do you have an address for her?"

Sissy flipped a few more pages and wrote down the address for the missing maid and handed it to me. "Just don't make a big deal out of telling people that I gave you the address." She asked.

"I won't tell a soul." I smiled and slipped her a ten and went out. I consulted my Palm TX map program and found the address, it was fairly close, so I headed over. I came to a group of apartments in clusters of eight, four down, four up. I could hear Mariachi music coming from an apartment somewhere; it reminded me of my apartment building when I lived here. I went to the ground floor door Sissy said was Marianna's apartment and knocked on it. After a minute or two a young boy opened the door, he was of Mexican decent and was just wearing shorts. I heard a woman yelling behind him that he wasn't supposed to open the door without her there. She was yelling in English, which was nice, since most of the Mexicans I had contact with back when I lived here all insisted on speaking Mexican. She opened the door wider and stood staring at me.

"Hi, my name is Jim Richards and I'm a private investigator." I handed her my card. "Are you Marianna Valez?"

She stared at the card briefly and said she was. I asked, "I just need to know if you remember the morning of February 10th at the motel you worked at, Starlight Motel, when a young woman said she was in a room where there was supposed to be a murder committed?"

Marianna just stared at me with a totally blank face, and then she said, "Yes, I remember that morning, I tried to tell the cop in charge that the woman had wandered in off the street and wouldn't leave the room I was cleaning, so I just left her there. The cop asked me to keep quiet about it till they got things straightened out. I said I wouldn't say anything about it. I never heard back from him."

"Why did you quit the job?" I asked.

"I got offered a job at the Venetian Hotel cleaning rooms, better pay and benefits."

"So you saw the woman go into the room and just sit?"

"Sort of, I was cleaning and went to get some more towels in the storage. When I came back she was sitting on the bed, just staring. It freaked me out, and she wouldn't respond to me, I figured she'd wake up eventually and get out, so I left her there."

"That explains it, thank you for your time." I smiled at the young boy, bent down and handed him a five dollar bill and left. I drove back to the office and explained to Lacey how she got across the street, she was sleepwalking.

"I never have been sleepwalking in my life, why did I start now?" she asked.

Penny said, "Probably from the shock of the murder, you were trying to run away from it."

Lacey took that in and smiled. "I hope it's over now, I don't like walking around in my night gown."

Penny and Lacey were laughing as I went to my office to call Lynn. When she came on I told her about my findings.

"Well that clears up that mystery. We still haven't found Mason; they got an APB out for him now. I'm trying to get a warrant for his phone records to see what he's been up to, but I'm sure he covered his tracks. I'll give you a call if anything turns up. Thanks for the info." We finished and I hung up.

I heard someone talking in the lobby and came out to see a woman standing at the counter talking to Penny. She looked to me as I came up and Penny said, "This is Mrs. Brantley, she'd like to talk to you." I thanked Penny and invited the woman to my office. She was a handsome black woman and looked to be in her seventies. She wasn't very tall, about five-three and had the look of a woman possessed. I motioned to my client chair and she sat.

"How did you find me Mrs. Brantley?" I asked.

"I talked to Captain Weber; he was a friend of my husband. He asked some detective if she knew where you were and told me."

"I see, what can I do for you Mrs. Brantley?"

"I want you to find the bastards who killed my husband and framed him to be a philanderer." She had a husky, smoking induced voice.

"You don't believe the preliminary report of the police that he was found with a hooker in a motel room?"

"My husband was a strict Baptist and a righteous man; he would have never been involved with a harlot in a motel. This was because he had the swing vote to keep prostitution out of the city. They have been fighting over it for a long time and he was the only hold out. Now they have that ass Muldoon in his seat and they probably will be passing the bill allowing hookers to work the city, with the new bill they have been trying to get passed."

"I know prostitution is illegal within the city limits but it goes on anyways. So why the interest in passing a bill allowing it legally?"

"Money of course. There are men who have hookers lined up for the taking if the bill passes. Imagine the casinos and the streets if the hookers and their pimps take over. Good people won't want to walk around our fair city for fear of being accosted by a hooker if they run the streets." She looked defiant and sat rigidly.

I was sure that the bill would have provisions to regulate the street walkers but it could get messy if the wrong people got into the pockets of certain officials, like Mason. "You want me to find his killers, is that what you want?"

"I want you to find whoever is behind this and bring them to justice. My Eldridge shouldn't have his name besmirched because of a few crooks. Can you help me Mr. Richards? I heard you have a good record behind you in solving crimes."

"Thank you Mrs. Brantley, I'll see what I can do for you."

"What do you charge for your investigations, Mr. Richards?"

"This one is on the house for you Mrs. Brantley, you've lost enough already."

She looked surprised and got a tear in her eye, "I loved my husband, we were married for over fifty years, just two crazy teenagers who should have known better, but we made it. Thank you Mr. Richards."

Sin City Murders

I gave her a tissue and a sheet of paper and asked her to write any information, names of people she thought may be involved, anything I may need to start my investigation. She took the paper and the pen I handed her and started to write whatever came to her mind that might help. She finished about ten minutes later and handed it back to me, I glanced at it and said I would be on it and would give her reports when I could.

"Please understand that I'm not a television detective, these things take time in real life so I'll let you know as soon as I have something and share it with the police."

"I know the real world, Mr. Richards, and will be patient. Thank you." She stood and I went around my desk to her, helping her out and I followed her to her car. She drove off and I went back in and smiled at Penny. "My first walk-in case." I said.

"Yep and you're making it a freebee, aren't you?"

"Hey, she's a nice lady and her husband is dead. She needs closure." I defended.

"I can see the only way I'm getting rich from this business is when you kick off."

"You keep that attitude and I'll never die."

"Ok, by me, we'll both live forever waiting for the other to go." She smiled and rubbed the butt of her gun now in a nice holster in her belt.

"Don't get any ideas." I warned her and went quickly to my office.

**

Chapter 16

I took the girls to a nice restaurant on Flamingo and we had a good sit down meal. Lacey was a little more alive now that things were coming together for her.

"I think that until the killers are found, you should probably keep staying at our place." Penny suggested. I think she just enjoyed having a female companion around, especially one who liked to swim.

"I don't want to be a bother, but I do feel safer there right now." She replied.

"I think it would be better, at least till we find out what happened to Mason, and since you can ID the killers now that you remember. Lynn wants you to come in tomorrow morning to go through the mug books to see if you spot anyone familiar." I said.

"I'll see what I can do; their faces are getting more prominent the more I think about them. I pretended to be drugged but I peeked whenever I could. I think I could spot them in the book."

"Good, then we can hopefully track them down and get to the bottom of it."

Our meal came and we ate with gusto, enjoying the fine cuisine and I even had a draft beer. We finished and left after getting the car and heading back home. I was now being cautious about anyone tailing me and watched my mirror frequently. I pulled into the drive and let Penny, Lacey and Willy out and put the car away. I went in after Penny had unlocked the door and I went straight to the kitchen to check the security. There had been no intruders while we were gone. It was nice to have motion sensor cameras around the house to pick up any activity, gave me a good feeling.

Penny and Lacey were already in their swimsuits and flopping around the pool. Willy was hiding behind the curtain of the patio door, shaking. I picked him up and we went out to the pool after a brief stop to feed the fish. I called Penny over and asked if Willy had ever been in the pool. She said he hadn't and I threw him in close to Penny. She looked shocked and grabbed for him but he came up and was paddling to beat hell towards her. She actually laughed at the sight of the tiny dog coming towards her. She got hold of him and held him up as he squirmed in her arms. He was squiggling so much that Penny had to release him and he took off again paddling in the water.

"See, he didn't know what to expect so I gave him a nudge. I've heard dogs are natural swimmers so he just needed to be introduced to it." I said as Penny was carefully watching Willy who was now paddling around her looking very happy. He went down in a dive and came back up spitting water, so Penny took him and put him on the ground. "Let's not over do it." Penny said and started to back away when Willy lunged into the water again. I thought I had created a monster. I told Penny to keep an eye on him and went back into the house to my home office and sat at the laptop. I worked on my story for a bit to get my mind off the case, then sat back thinking about Mrs. Brantley.

I took the paper from my shirt pocket that she had written on and it had a few names and their positions in Vegas. A couple councilmen and Muldoon was featured at the top. Maybe I should drop in on him to get his take on the crime. I pulled my cell phone and called Lynn. She came on after a couple rings and sounded weary.

"Hey Jim, just finishing a long day here, I'm beat and we still haven't put a dent in finding Mason. Whatcha need?"

"What do you know about Freddie Muldoon?"

"The new councilman who took over for Brantley, not much, he just suddenly popped into the political scene by vote of the other councilmen. I hear is a hardcore liberal and proponent for prostitution. Why?"

"I got a visit from Mrs. Brantley today asking me to find her husband's killers. She mentioned him, I know nothing about him."

"Do a Google search; he's all over there about his plans to revitalize Las Vegas. I don't like the guy from what I hear. Weber asked me what your address was, for a friend of his, I presume it was her."

"Yep, she dropped his name. I'm going to look into Muldoon and find out what his stance is on murder. I'll let you know what I find. What's Deacon up to?"

"You know I think he would be better off following you around if you don't mind. He has been awful mopey lately having to chase after gangbangers; I can assign him as your protection, that may perk him up."

"I have no problem with that; it would be good to work with him again." I smiled remembering all the running around we did in the past chasing crime. "I'll be bringing in Lacey in the morning to go through the mug books, so Deacon and I can start plotting then."

"That works for me, see you in the morning then." We finished and I looked out the window to the pool and could see three heads floating in the pool now. I just hope Willy knows enough to swim carefully.

~~*~~

Mosh and Willis crept up to the ranch style house and looked into a window on the side. Mosh could see Mason sitting in a chair in what looked to be a living room. They couldn't see anyone else in the house, so they went around to the back. The door was open to the backyard and there was no one there either. They slowly went in and snuck up behind Mason just when they heard a clicking sound behind them; Mosh turned his head and was looking down the barrel of a shotgun pointing at both of them. Mason jumped up when he heard the click and found his girlfriend holding the shotgun on the two men. Mason had his service revolver drawn and said, "This isn't a good move guys."

A half hour later, Mason came into the office of the fat man followed by Mosh and Willis both with handcuffs on. Mason pulled his revolver on the fat man and said, "Don't fuck with me, I'll blow you to hell if you try anything again, understand me? And don't send idiots to do a man's job." Mason's girlfriend was undoing the cuffs and pushed the two men to the side of the room, she had a Luger aimed at them.

"Mason, let's be reasonable, I need you. You don't really think these two dumb fucks would try to kill you?"

"My friends and associates don't sneak up behind me with guns drawn." He barked.

Willis spoke, "We were just being cautious about coming in, didn't want to find anyone else in the house other than Mason. Honest."

Mason turned his gun on Willis and said to never enter his house again. Then turned to the fat man and said, "Remember this, I'm watching you now. Don't fuck with me."

~~**~~

Early the next morning I awoke, thankfully hearing no alarms in the night. I got up and Penny went out for a quick swim followed by the water dog. Lacey came out to join them and they did a few laps and got out. I came out to see that Penny was spinning around the stripper pole giving Lacey a few pointers about the art of pole dancing.

"Thinking of changing professions?" I asked Lacey. She giggled and said she had no intentions of stripping for men, not her idea of a good job.

They went in to get dressed and I took the Crown Vic out again and waited for them. We arrived at the Metro precinct around 9 A.M. and found Lynn talking to some man in a well-tailored suit. We stood back then Lynn saw us and brought the man over.

"Jim this is Assistant District Attorney Ralph Marley, he's going to supervise Lacey checking the mug books. So if we can get started." She led us to a room down the hall and we went in. Deacon was there getting all the mugshot books set out on the table for Lacey. "Okay, Lacey if you can just take your time and look at each man carefully, maybe you'll see someone you recognize."

Lacey sat and started to go through the books, as Deacon asked me to follow him. We went to the break room and Deacon bought me a hot chocolate and a coffee for him from the machine. We sat at one of the tables and he asked me what I had come up with so far. I told him everything that had happened in the last couple days and about Brantley's wife requesting help.

He sat listening and said, "I know of Muldoon, he's a hard ass about wanting his own way. This town just isn't good enough for him, he wants to change things. I think he just has cash on his mind, but if you want to go talk to him, I've got your back."

"Great, when do you want to start?" I asked.

"Now's as good a time as any, he's in his office in the city hall, I called ahead to be sure." He smiled and we got up. I went to tell Penny we were going and to call me if Lacey finds anything. She kissed me and said to be careful. Deacon said he would drive, and we should take an unmarked car since it would be better for parking around City Hall. They don't ticket cop cars, he laughed.

We pulled out of the motor pool with a black Dodge Charger police interceptor, it was available and Deacon wanted to drive the beast. I joked that we weren't chasing anyone and he said you never can tell.

We got to City Hall and he parked in an area for police cars and we went in to find Muldoon's office. We went in and the secretary asked us what we needed. I asked if we could see Muldoon and we showed our badges. Mine was still from Michigan, but no one ever looked close enough to read it. She said to wait and called him.

His door opened and out came the fattest man I had seen in a long time.

**

Chapter 17

Fat Bastard, came to my mind. You know, the humongously huge criminal from the "Austin Powers" movies. This guy was a mountain of fat and I couldn't figure out how he could stay upright. If he fell on his side he would roll.

"Gentlemen, you may come in." He said with a flourish of his hand attached to a side of beef. Luckily he moved from the door so we could walk in and he went to sit on the oversized chair behind his desk. "Now what can I do for Vegas' finest?"

"Mr. Muldoon, this gentleman is LVMPD Detective Frank DeAngelo and my name is Jim Richards and I'm a private investigator. I'm helping a young woman to find out who tried to frame her for the murder of Eldridge Brantley." I figured I'd throw my cards out and see what expression he had on his face.

His face didn't twitch a muscle and he said, "I thought he was murdered by a hooker?"

"Well, it was set up to look that way; we have other information that there may have been a conspiracy to unseat the councilman by killing him." He still didn't move a muscle, good poker face, or the fat had hardened in his face so he couldn't make an expression. "We were wondering if you may have heard anything to corroborate this assumption?"

"No, sir, I haven't any idea of this so called plot. Do you have any suspects?" He was sweating a bit now, but it was warm in the office.

"Not at the moment, but we just wondered if you could help, seeing as you did take the former councilman's seat." Yeah, three of them I thought.

"No I can't help you, but I will keep this in mind if I hear anything. You know how gossip goes on in the world of politics." He wiped his face with a towel he had on his desk.

"You should have air conditioning in here, sir." Deacon offered.

"I'm not a cold weather person, Detective; I prefer warmth, even if it has its side effects."

"Did you know Brantley, Mr. Muldoon?" I asked.

"I had met him a few times, yes I knew him briefly."

"Did he seem the type to go off with a hooker?"

"I can't speak for the late councilman's predilections. He may have been a closet sex maniac."

"You are a proponent for prostitution in the city are you not?"

"I have my reasons for supporting the bill. Many men come here to gamble and do business. They should have the pleasure of female companionship, yes, I'm for it."

"Mr. Brantley was against it, wasn't he? With him gone now the bill can pass easily. That seems a coincidence don't you think?"

"Yes, it is an unfortunate coincidence but life deals us all forms of coincidences doesn't it?"

"The murder of the councilman by a hooker doesn't help the cause to get the bill passed, does it now?"

"I am sure that the incident is just one minor cog in a bigger picture. This shouldn't hurt the bill's passage."

"What business were you in before you took the council seat, Mr. Muldoon."

"I own the Black Slipper saloon in the north end."

"Isn't that a conflict of interest, owning a strip joint and being on the council to vote for the bill to allow prostitution?"

"I gave up my interest in the club to my nephews when I was asked to join the council, so not to taint the vote."

"That was simple; I suppose you have no interest in regaining the club after the bill passes?"

"Mr. Richards, I'm sorry but I have meetings to attend. I gave you the time you wanted but now I must insist we finish this. Please find your way out, as I have some phone calls to make before my meetings. Thank you for coming and I hope I may have been of some help."

We stood and I turned without shaking the hand he extended. I didn't like the man and wondered how he could have gotten the backing to get on the council. He had to have people in his pocket. We went out of the office and when we were in the hallway I told Deacon what I was thinking.

"I agree, he is not the type I would vote for if he was running for dog catcher. Shall we go shake up a few more councilmen." He grinned and I said let's do that.

My cell phone rang and it was Penny. I answered and she told me that Lacey found one photo of one of the men. A guy named Marko Willis, a felon with a long record and who was presently out on parole. The DA had the police put an APB for Willis and time would tell if they found him. I thanked her and said I had an interesting story about Muldoon to tell her when I got back. I asked her if she could see if Lynn could get some information on Muldoon's holdings on a strip club and who his nephews are since they now owned the club. She said she'd take care of it and we hung up.

"Lacey ID'd one of the men; they have an APB out for him. Let's go finish our tree shaking and go back."

We went to the office of Dick Hudsen and we were greeted by him at his door as he was just getting back from lunch. He invited us in after we introduced ourselves and we went to sit. I explained about our mission for Lacey and he expressed his sadness for the late councilman.

"Mr. Hudsen, do you have any idea why Mr. Muldoon was brought in on the council?" I asked.

"You mean Man Mountain Muldoon? I was against it. I was one of half of the council against the prostitution bill, but somehow we were out voted by the other half and a few of my people to bring Muldoon in. I frankly think its money, greed and Muldoon has something to blackmail a number of the members. I don't indulge in his sex games so I guess he couldn't get anything on me." He offered some coffee, we said no and he continued. "All of the council was mixed on the bill and Eldridge was the guiding force against it. When I heard he was murdered in a motel by a hooker, I knew something had to be wrong, but how do you prove it? The cops were most likely in Muldoon's pocket so the bill may pass now. Poor Eldridge, he must be spinning in his grave."

I looked to Deacon, he shrugged and we thanked Hudsen for his time and we left. I said one more councilman and we can call it a day.

We next went to the office of Morris Lane, and found him exercising on a stationary bike. "I don't get enough time out of the office and at home so this is my daily routine to keep the body in shape, now what can I do for you two?"

Again I explained our mission and he smiled and sat at his desk motioning us to sit. "Mr. Lane, what is your take on Freddie Muldoon?"

"Why, do you suspect him of something?"

"Just asking questions, not saying he has done anything wrong." Deacon spoke.

Lane was starting to act nervous and seemed to want to be somewhere else at the moment. "Mr. Lane, does Mr. Muldoon have something on you that you may not want public?" I asked hoping to stir him up.

"Are you insinuating that he may be blackmailing me? That's outrageous! He's a fine man and he has good ideas to improve the city. Back when the corporations that were running the town tried to make a Disney Land out of it, thinking they could bring in families, but that didn't work, so now we have to get back to the Sin City theme that draws in the money people. Muldoon has the right ideas to do so."

I could see this guy was a fan of Muldoon and probably wouldn't cooperate so I nodded to Deacon and we gave our thanks and left. Back out on the street, I said, "That must have stirred up a few people, wouldn't you say?"

"Yeah, I'd like to be in on the phone calls Muldoon had to make, probably calling in his men to cover his ass. I hope we can get a link from Willis to Muldoon, it sure would help. Shall we retire to the station?" Deacon asked.

We hopped in the Charger and drove back down to Metro and put the car back. I found Penny and Lacey in Lynn's office and Deacon went off to check on his gangbangers who he had stewing in interrogation for the last two hours. Deacon smiled and said, "They should be ripe to talk."

Lynn said the DA was pleased that Lacey was able to ID at least one of the men, it would help. I asked if she needed us any further, she said no so we left. I took the girls and dog to Sonic's again and we ate in the car.

It was now just getting dark as we came along the road to our home. From a distance I could see the front porch motion controlled lights were on. I turned into the drive but stopped by the road. I told Penny and Lacey to stay in the car and have her .38 handy. I went around the side of the house between the guesthouse and the main house carefully looking around the corner.

While I was checking the rear of the house, Lacey's car door suddenly flew open and she was pulled out. Penny quickly opened her door and stood holding her gun down behind the opened rear car door since the man had Lacey in a head lock with his gun on her head. He said not to do anything stupid and to go into the house. Penny was waiting for an opening, then Lacey was struggling to get away and turned her body just enough to open the man up on his gun side. Penny brought the .38 up and fired at the assailant's gun arm causing him to release Lacey and stagger back. His arm hung limp and he had dropped the gun and turned to run. Penny walked around Lacey, took aim and fired at him in the leg. He went down.

I had heard the first shot and came flying around just before the second shot put him down. I ran up to him and put my knee in his back holding him on the ground and yelled to Penny to call the police. I bent down to his ear and said, "You shouldn't have messed with my wife, fool."

**

Chapter 18

Lacey had identified the man as Willis, while Penny had called Lynn and explained the situation. Lynn called dispatch to send out a patrol car and an EMT while she was on her way. The medical tech said both wounds were superficial, just enough to disable the man, but not enough to do any damage. Lynn looked to Penny and said she was simply amazed. Penny just grinned. I sat on the trunk of my car holding Willy, and watching it all take place and wondering what other talents my wife had.

"Well, we'll take Willis back to a cell and interrogate him in the morning; I'll need Lacey to press charges on him for attempted kidnap and threat to do bodily harm. She was a witness in the motel crime so we'll formally charge him with Brantley's murder. He will have some explaining to do." She smiled at Penny and said, "I'm glad you're on our side, Dead Eye."

Sin City Murders

~~*~~

Buck was at the Ford dealership by nine in the evening with his men waiting for the manager to show. Mac Knight was explaining the layout of the property since he had patrolled the lot when he worked for Retcho. He was explaining the trouble areas of the place when a car drove up, it was the manager. Carl Davis came up to Buck and they shook hands, asking if Buck's men were ready for the task.

"My men are as ready as they'll ever be, this is Mac Knight and he is familiar with the property so we've been getting a little lay of the land." Davis acknowledged Mac and handed Buck an envelope with the signed agreements for guard service Buck had prepared. Davis took a few minutes to explain to Buck's men what the dealership expected and then said he'd walk them around the lot to show the troubled area where they had problems before. About a half hour later they were back at the start and Buck told Mac to get the men going.

Buck waited for the men to go off then turned to Davis and said, "There may be a small problem. We had a threat the other day about working here. We did some checking and it looks like it came from Retcho. Did you part their company friendly or just drop them?"

"We had some problems with them, guards sleeping and not watching the property properly. We had warned them a number of times but they took it rather belligerently and we let it go since there weren't any other guard services handy and available. When you showed up it was about time for a change, so we let them go." Davis explained.

"Well, we are expecting possible trouble so be warned. I'm going to sit in tonight and help watch the place and to familiarize myself with the area. I hope nothing goes on, but we'll be ready."

Davis thanked Buck and handed him the keys to the gates and buildings. Buck thanked Davis and he drove off. Buck turned to see Mac coming back to him and they stood looking at the cars all lined up in many rows. It was a huge place and would need to be watched closely, so Buck told Mac to watch the back half with the guards and he'd watch the front. Buck went to his car and got out the walkie-talkies he brought and gave one to Mac. They tested them and split up. Buck stood looking at the sales room in front of him thinking about the dealership he left in Michigan. He smiled and was happy.

Sin City Murders

~~*~~

We staggered tiredly into the house and Penny fell on the couch. Lacey had gone off to her guesthouse and I reset the alarms around the property. I reviewed the video from the motion sensor cameras and played back the incident with Penny shooting Willis. I would make a copy of the video for Lynn to use against Willis.

I grabbed a couple of beers from the fridge and went to the couch, Penny already had the TV on to another comedy we liked and we sat quietly watching the show. We were talked out and wanted mindless entertainment to get away from the harsh realities of life. After two hours of mindless entertainment we went to the bedroom for mindless sex. Penny took her frustrations out on me; I will say it was very good.

We cuddled and then I said, "When I shot Morgan and killed him, it bothered me, but I realized he was evil and sort of justified it. I still have the occasional nightmare about it, but I'll survive. You shot Nick North that time we were out here and you never spoke about how you felt shooting a man, even though he lived through it. Now you've shot another man and I need to know if you're okay with it?"

She hugged me a little tighter, "I shot Nick to protect you, and I shot Willis to protect Lacey. They both were criminals; I have no problem with it. Well, one maybe, I probably should have killed them both, but I would have had a problem with that, so I didn't."

"You are amazing."

"About time you realized that."

We slept well, and were up early. Penny had rousted Lacey out of bed and they took their morning swim joined by Willy. I called Buck to see how his first night went at the dealership.

"Jimmy, I was just going to take a nap. Done for the night and no problems, but then I had four men watching the place. Once I'm confident that we won't be disturbed, I'll just have the two men on. How did Lacey do with the mugshots?"

"She ID'd one of the men, name's Marko Willis, but we caught him last night when he attempted to grab Lacey in our own drive. Penny took him down with two well placed shots from her new .38, he'll live to talk. Lynn is going to interrogate him this morning so I'm trying to get everyone ready to go."

"Good thing you got Penny the gun, tell her I'm proud of her. Well, let me know how the questioning goes. I'm going to sleep for a couple hours to recharge and I'll be in the office the rest of the day. If you need me just call," he said as we finished and hung up.

Penny came through the kitchen followed by a wet Willy. She laughed and said, "I was having a problem keeping Willy out of the pool, he was even diving down now. I'll have to get him a little snorkel and mask if he keeps this up." I laughed and asked if they could get dressed so we could go watch Willis get interrogated. Penny said Lacey went to get dressed and she would be ready in about fifteen minutes. It always amazed me how she could get ready so fast. I guess television does that to you, having to get ready for her shows.

We arrived at Metro PD around 10 A.M. and Lynn took us to interrogation. ADA Ralph Marley was in the room and asked Lacey to look at the man and confirm he was in the motel that night Brantley was murdered. Lacey didn't hesitate; she said he was one of the men. Marley smiled and stood back from the window. I let Lacey and Penny take the two chairs in the room watching the two way glass to the room where Willis sat fidgeting in his chair. His arm was wrapped in a bandage at the shoulder but we could see he could move his arm well enough to take a drink from a paper cup in front of him. Lynn said it was showtime and left us. She went into the interrogation room and stood for a minute before sitting. She was studying Willis, and making him nervous. For a cold blooded killer, he wasn't very tough.

Lynn just started to talk when the door opened and in walked Captain Weber. Lynn looked surprised as he came to the table leaning over and said quietly, but loud enough for us to hear over the speakers in the observation room, "Brantley was my friend. We will pull you and anyone else down, be sure of it. I'm going to be watching you now. Count on it."

He stood and smiled at Lynn saying, "Good work Detective. Carry on," and he walked out. Willis got wide eyed and looked to Lynn and asked, "who the hell was that?" Lynn didn't break a smile and said, "That was Captain Weber, head of this division. Not a man you want on your bad side."

"Look Willis we know you are a small cog in this wheel, we want the people higher up. We suspect that Muldoon is in this somehow, what do you think?"

He took a stone faced look and sat back. "I'm not putting my head in a noose to give you anyone. The people behind this have a long reach." Then he went quiet.

"Do you know Mosh Gower, Muldoon's nephew?" He said nothing.

"Okay, shall we discuss Mason? How is he in this?"

"Like I said, a long reach."

"Willis, you have been positively identified as one of the murderers of Eldridge Brantley. It will be proven in court and you'll do a long stretch. Give us some names and maybe we can make it easier on you."

"Long reach," was all he said.

He just sat with his eyes fixed in the mirror now and Lynn sat back. "You also have attempted kidnap with intent to do bodily harm. More piling up on you, let's make it easy for you; give us something to go on, give us just one name."

"My lawyer, that's the only name I'll give you."

Lynn got up and called for the officers waiting to take him back to his cell. As he was standing, Lynn she said to him, "I'll be sure to let Muldoon know you ratted him out."

He stopped and looked at her, "That would be my death sentence. You think you can protect me from him or that cop he has on his payroll? Good luck." He went to the guard and they left.

**

Chapter 19

"Well it wasn't a confession but it confirms that Muldoon and Mason were involved," Lynn said as she entered the observation room. "Now we need to see if we can get them to talk, if we could only find Mason. We can bring in Muldoon since we know where his is, but from what Deacon told me, we'd need a forklift to bring him in." She smiled and turned to Marley, "What's your take on it?"

"All circumstantial so far, without hard evidence we can't touch Muldoon. If Mason were to come forward and give us something then maybe we'd have enough to prosecute. Wish I could give you more." He excused himself and left.

Lynn just looked frustrated and asked us to go back to her office. "So we can't touch Muldoon without some hard evidence for his involvement in the murder. Was this really the purpose for putting Muldoon in office, to pass a bill legalizing prostitution? It goes on all the time, legalizing it just makes it okay to solicit on the streets and in the hotels. But the hotels won't tolerate it and they can make it off limits to hookers anyways. There has to be more to this than just prostitution."

"You said Muldoon had a plan to spice up Vegas, could this just be the tip of the iceberg?" I asked.

"Could be, he may be just starting to get his clutches on the reigns of the city. I hope we can get Willis or Mason to talk."

We were relaxing when the door opened and one of the officers who took Willis to his cell said, "Lieutenant, Willis asked me to give you a message. He said that Mason was at his girlfriend's home and he wasn't going down alone for this."

Lynn asked the officer if he knew Mason, he said he didn't. Lynn was smiling now and picked up her phone. She called a friend in North Vegas PD and asked if he knew Mason. He did. Lynn put it on speaker phone.

"Do you know if he has a girlfriend?" She asked.

"Yeah, she was one of his busts a year ago, some hooker trying to go good now. He's keeping her on a short leash."

"Do you know where her crib is?"

"Not exactly, but I heard they have a place off Cheyenne, just east of Buffalo. You may be able to check her priors for the address, name's May Bartlet."

"Thanks Steve." She disconnected and turned to her computer and did some typing till the screen came up with a window that showed the woman's face. "Not very glamorous is she." She saw the arrest report with Mason's signature and she noted the address then called North Vegas PD and asked for Captain Sustaine. He came on and Lynn flipped on the speaker phone again.

"Lynn, what can I do for you?" He asked.

"You want Mason, I want Mason, I got a location but it's in your jurisdiction, can we work together on this?"

"Mason has been in this department for over twelve years, I find it hard to believe he's in this, but give me the address and we'll talk."

Lynn read off the address and then said, "We have sort of a confirmation that Mason may have been involved in the murder of Brantley and is tied into Muldoon. I just want him to confirm Muldoon's guilt so we can take him. You can have Mason from there for whatever you can get on him."

Sustaine was silent for a moment then said, "You got it, want in on the bust?"

"If you don't mind."

"Nope, just bring your vest, Mason's a cowboy and will shoot if cornered. Hopefully he won't shoot cops but we don't know. I'll call for a warrant and will meet you here, then we'll head out."

They finished and Lynn called Weber to apprise him of the situation, Weber said to go for it. We all filed out and I took my team to my car with a warning from Lynn to keep back if it goes bad. Lynn and Deacon went in her car and drove out and up to join North Vegas PD, finding Sustaine in the parking lot getting his men situated. He was setting up the attack on the house while waiting for the warrant. They got the papers delivered by a courier and Sustaine said it was a go. We all drove out to the address Lynn had, and we pulled down the street from where the house was. Sustaine had four patrol cars and a van of SWAT officers all pulling up to the property.

They all converged on the house, sitting in the middle of a large piece of property. There were two cars in the drive, we presumed to be Mason's and his girlfriend. The men had the house surrounded and Sustaine had a bullhorn and called for Mason to come out peacefully. There was nothing for a moment then the front door opened and a woman stepped out with her hands up. Two of the SWAT men ran forward and took her to the line of cars by the road. Captain Sustaine came to her and asked where Mason was; she looked to him and said, "He's in the house. He didn't want me hurt so he sent me out. He's not going to give in."

Sustaine got back on the bullhorn and asked Mason to give up. Mason called from an open window, "Forget it Captain. I got too many enemies if I go in."

"So you want to die here is that it, Don? I've worked with you too long to let this go bad. Let's talk and I'll do what I can for you."

"Captain, you don't understand what these people can do. I go in and I'm dead, either way I'm dead. Be a nice guy and let me skate, I'll be out of the state and no one will ever see me again."

"Damn it Don, you know it doesn't work that way. I will guarantee your safety, you know me, I will."

It was too quiet. Sustaine got back on the horn and said, "Look Don, I'll get you out of the county, far enough away and quietly so no one will know where you are, we just want the people who are behind this. You give us them and I'll hide you out till they are all taken down, what do you say?"

It was quiet again and Mason yelled, "Get everyone out of here and you take me alone, one other cop and I'll come in but not to the precinct. Take me to where ever you can put me safely, I'll agree to that."

Sustaine stood mulling it over. He turned to Lynn and said, "I know that man, he's a good cop. Maybe he went wrong, but I would trust him. I think maybe if you'd go with me being from Metro, he may relax." Lynn said she just wanted Muldoon, and if Mason can finger him, she would help.

"Mason." Sustaine called again, "I got Lieutenant Lynn Carter here from Metro, she needs help taking down Freddie Muldoon. She will come with me and we will take you to safety. Is that good enough?"

Mason was quiet again, then said, "Get everyone away and gone. Then we'll talk in here. Let May come with you."

Sustaine turned to his lieutenant and said to get everyone out of here. The lieutenant asked if he really trusted Mason. The Captain thanked him for his concern and said to move now. He went off and yelled for everyone to scatter and go back to the precinct.

Lynn told Deacon to tell me to go back home for now and she'd call when it was over. Deacon looked concerned and told her so, quietly. She told him she'd be all right and to wait for her at her office. He came to my car and told me what was going on, I said I'd be in my office and we drove off. Deacon took a look back to Lynn standing alone with Sustaine and gave her a little wave and got into his car and drove off.

Sustaine said he would go in first and told Lynn to watch May until he was sure it was good. They walked up to the door and it opened. Mason was standing there with his hands up. Sustaine went to him and checked for weapons, then relaxed. May ran to Mason and they held on to each other and then we all went into the house.

Mason sat May down and turned to Sustaine and Lynn. "I got into this and made a mistake. I am in too far to get out, unless a whole lot of people give up or die. You don't know how far reaching this goes. Muldoon is just the beard for the real bad guys, he's just a fat fuck who thinks he runs things but he's just a puppet for the real criminals. I can't give you them, I don't even know, but Muldoon is behind the murder of Brantley, he and his stupid nephew, Mosh Gower. There's a professional hitman named Willis who they brought in on it also."

Lynn interrupted and said they had Willis in a cell at Metro, and then she told him what happened. He smiled and said, "That's rich, him being taken down by a woman. Well, he's just one of many who are in the army of crime bent on turning Vegas into a real Sin City. Muldoon is just a figure head, the devil is running it all now."

**

Chapter 20

Sustaine called a friend he knew in the U.S. Marshals office in Boulder City and explained the situation, Mason just sat listening. Lynn was watching him and saw a fear in his expression that made her wonder how powerful this crime organization could be. The Marshal said he could put Mason in protective custody and would have someone pick him up. Sustaine said to be sure he was watched carefully, he still is involved in a crime yet not established. Sustaine gave the directions and hung up.

"Don, I hope you aren't into this too deeply, I don't want to see you go down. What do you know?"

He sat for a moment thinking, then said, "I got in because I took a bribe to look the other way on the Brantley murder. When that girl came out of left field and reported the incident I was asked to discredit her. They didn't want her dead because that would draw attention, so I just fudged the reports to keep her out of it. If she hadn't failed to commit suicide this would all just have gone away, but that PI got involved and things were going wrong. I just hid out; I wasn't sure how far it would go.

Muldoon sent his men to do a hit on me but we stopped them and threw them back at Muldoon."

"Don, this isn't you. What got into your head man?"

"I was in deep with the bookies, I needed the money and Muldoon provided it. I screwed up; I'll take the crime but not the hit."

"Bookies? Why didn't you go to the sports book in any casino?"

"They won't take my marker, they want cash up front. I didn't have it. I made a number of bad choices on games and lost my shirt. I couldn't pay and Muldoon is in on the illegal gambling around Vegas. So he made me a deal I had to take."

Sustaine just stood quietly looking at Mason. "I'll do my damnedest to go to bat for you, but you have to cooperate Don. Get out of town and give your deposition to the DA and we'll see what we can do."

"Thanks Captain." Mason said quietly.

They were just standing waiting for the Marshals when things went crazy. The walls were suddenly being razed by automatic gun fire and everyone dropped to the floor. Mason was covering his girlfriend and they just hung low. Not being able to fight against the powerful weapons, they hid behind chairs and tables hoping the Marshals would arrive soon.

Sin City Murders

Suddenly the auto gun fire stopped and they heard small hand gun fire. Sustaine went to a window and did a quick peek out and saw a Vegas police car with flashers going and there was firing coming from the car. Sustaine and Lynn went to the door and opened it carefully with guns drawn. They could see the cop car but not the cop firing at the van with the men who assaulted the house. A couple more shots later and it was over. Lynn could see Deacon stand up beside his car and she went out with Sustaine. Lynn ran up to Deacon, he told her that he parked down the road, he wasn't going to leave her alone and when he saw the van speed up and two men jumped out with automatic weapons, he drove up. They were concentrating on blasting the house and they didn't see him pull up and he began firing on them.

Sustaine suddenly realized that Mason was still in the house and went back followed by Lynn and Deacon. Mason was still on the floor holding his girlfriend. She had blood coming from her mouth and she looked limp. Mason was crying and looked up to Sustaine, "Fuck the protection, this is personal now. Take me in; I'm ready to take these bastards down."

A half hour later, the medics had the two shooters and the girl's body in black bags and were transporting them back to the Medical

Examiner's office. Mason was banging on the top of Sustaine's car, he turned to Sustaine and said, "I want Muldoon's hide. I want the pigs who pull his chains. I want someone to suffer for this." He put his head on the car and cried. Lynn felt bad for him, he wasn't a bad guy, he was just pulled into a bad situation. She looked to Deacon and said, "You watch your ass, do you hear?" Deacon smiled and said he would.

The Marshals had shown up and Sustaine explained what had happened and that Mason had changed his decision and was going to stay in Vegas now. They said no problem and went off.

~~*~~

We were sitting in the office wondering what was going on at the house. I worried about Lynn but realized I couldn't worry about every cop who put their lives in jeopardy going out to something as simple as a pull over and being shot by a drug dealer. The world was not a good place. I looked to Penny and Lacey sitting at the desk playing with Willy. I would never let anything ever happen to Penny and as long as Lacey was in our care, she would be protected also. My phone rang and I answered, it was Lynn. She told me what had happened, I was glad she was all right, but upset that

Mason's girlfriend was killed. Lynn said to keep a close eye on Lacey now that she is a witness to the murder of Brantley. There are more people involved with this than previously thought. I said I would, hung up and went to Buck's office.

"Hey buddy, what's up?" Buck asked.

I told him what had happened and asked if he could do me a favor. He said, "Talk to me."

"I want to hire a couple of your guards to sit and watch my property. I'll pay them for their time. I want men who are certified to carry and not afraid to fire on the bad guys, carefully."

He smiled and said he'd do the job himself along with Mac Knight. "When and how long?" He asked.

"Start tonight. I'll set you up with the place to watch from and what to expect. Bring lots of ammo," I said and told him I would let him know more later. I went back to Penny and asked her to follow me.

We went outside to the front of the building, it was now about ninety degrees outside and I said I would make this quick. I explained what had happened at the house we had left and she was upset by the outcome. I said that I was going to have Buck watch our house until we get this taken care of. Lacey was the only link to put away Muldoon and his men, so she was in extreme danger.

She looked at me and said, "I knew you would get us in a dangerous situation. I know death likes to follow you, but now I have my .38 and I'll be damned if anyone hurts Lacey, or you." I kissed her and she said it was hot out here, so we went in. It was getting late so I told Buck that we were finished and gathered ourselves up and left.

We drove back to our house and shortly after Buck pulled up followed by Mac. I invited them in and explained to them how I wanted the surveillance to go. I showed them the surveillance cameras and where I wanted them to cover and where they could sit to watch. Lacey was pleased that Mac was going to be around to guard her, she smiled and thanked him. Mac went a few shades of red and said she was welcome. I suspected Mac had a little crush on Lacey and she seemed to not object to the attention from him. I told Buck that was all I had and then he and Mac went out to position themselves to watch the house.

I had hidden them so if anyone came to kill us, Buck and Mac would be aware of the attack. The girls went to the pool to swim and relax, I had insisted on it. Willy was in his glory swimming in the pool and I sat and watched them all splashing around and enjoying the cool water. After a while I went to the front of the house and called Buck on the walkie-talkie that he gave me and told him we were going into the house for the night and asked if he needed anything. Buck said he was good and Mac called from his walkie-talkie saying he was ready for anything. I thanked them and said we were settling in for the night.

I went in and said that I wanted Lacey to sleep in our spare guestroom tonight. She had no problem with it and went to get her bed clothes, changing from her swimsuit. Penny had talked to her by the pool and explained what could happen. Lacey was surprised that there was so much going on in her life. She said that she would be more aware of things going on around her and I said we would be watching her. We all went to bed but I couldn't sleep.

Around 4 A.M. I heard a commotion out front and wondered why the property alarms hadn't gone off. I got dressed quickly and went to the front window and saw Buck out by the road with a man on the ground. I shut down the alarm system, went out to them, just as Mac came running over.

"He came walking down the road from a car he parked," Buck said and pointed to a car down the road, "I watched him come up here and he had this with him." He handed me a bag, I looked in and found enough dynamite to blow the whole house up. "The dumb shit was watching the house and I snuck up behind him and got the jump on him."

I bent down to the unconscious man and went through his pockets, found a wallet and looked at the driver's license. "Well, we have a celebrity, Mosh Gower, Muldoon's nephew."

**

Chapter 21

We had Mosh cuffed to a chair in the living room, he was still unconscious, and I called Lynn, hating to wake her so early. I explained what happened and where Mosh was now; she chuckled and said she'd be out in a short while. Mac had stayed outside to continue guarding as Buck and I stood watching the weasely looking man. Penny and Lacey were just now coming out of the bedrooms and Lacey got a shocked look on her face.

"That's him; he's the other man in the motel when Brantley was killed. Him and the guy in jail now." She said as she got her face real close to the still unconscious man. "Yep, it's him all right." She stood looking proud.

"Well, the plot progresses." I said as Penny came to me. She smiled and said we could let him loose so she could take some target practice on him. "I don't think so babe," I said.

I was wondering what Buck did to the guy for him be out so long and asked.

"I just came up behind him and coughed, he turned and I sucker punched him. He went down and here he sits."

"Well, we'll wait till Lynn gets here before we attempt to wake him." I said and went to the door as I heard a car pull up, it was Lynn and Deacon. "You made good time."

"Jim, its 5 A.M., there's not a lot of traffic out here this early." She went to Mosh and said, "So this is him. We don't have him on file so I've never seen his face. Ugly isn't he?"

I brought out a spray bottle of water that Penny used to mist the few real plants she had and spritzed his face. He started to move his head and was blinking his eyes, then found he was staring into the face of Lynn, bending down to him. He looked shocked.

"Good morning princess," Lynn smiled. "Do you know how much trouble you are in? Carrying dynamite to commit a felony and murder. Plus I have a witness who places you at the murder of Eldridge Brantley. How's that for bad luck?"

He didn't say anything; he was just looking at the floor now. Lynn stood up and said, "I called a patrol car to come get him and they'll take him in to share a cell with Willis. Maybe they'll kill each other and save the city the money to take them to trial."

I had to laugh at the panicked look on Mosh's face when Lynn mentioned Willis. Buck got a call on his cell and he went outside to take it. He stood talking for a couple minutes then came back in looking concerned and said he had to leave. He called to Mac on the walkie-talkie and said to come back. I asked what was wrong and he said they had a small problem at the dealership last night; he had to go check it out. I asked if he needed any help, he thanked me but said I had more important things to worry about. I told him I worry about him too, he said he appreciated that but needed to take care if it himself. Mac came up to the house and the two of them left.

~~*~~

Buck and Mac arrived at the dealership and saw the two guards with another man standing in the middle of the lot. They went to them and one of the guards introduced the morning repair shop manager, Brian. He came in to work and shortly after one of the guards heard glass breaking and drove around to find windshields on three of the Ford Explorers broken. Buck went to the car and examined the windshield and determined that it was shot by an air rifle. He looked in the direction of where the shots could have come from and went to the wall that bordered the lot. He stood up on the bumper of a car parked next to the wall and looked over. There was a ladder standing against the other side where the shooter could have stood.

As they were looking over the wall, a police car pulled up and two big cops got out coming to the guards. One of the guards told Buck he called the police to report the incident, Buck said that was good. The cops looked the situation over and checked the ladder and determined that it was vandalism. Buck thought to himself these guys are geniuses.

A few minutes later, Carl Davis drove up and they explained the situation to him. Buck said to the manager and the cops, "I said that Retcho had made threats but this is just childish and stupid."

One on the cops asked if they had proof that it was Retcho who threatened them and Buck said they had the call recorded and the number came from Retcho. The cop made a written report and asked if he could have a copy of the recording sent to him, Buck said he would take care of it.

Nothing more they could do so the cops left and Carl told Buck that they wouldn't hold it against his men since Buck did warn him. This was a deliberate attempt to discredit Buck's guards. Buck told Carl that he'd take care of it with Retcho.

~~*~~

Lacey had to sign a few papers saying she witnessed Mosh being in the motel room when Brantley was murdered. We were sitting in Lynn's office and had spent the better part of the morning waiting. Lynn had Mosh processed through booking and was going to question him shortly. She finally asked us to follow, taking us to the observation room, the DA was there to watch and Lynn went into interrogation.

"Mosh, how are you this morning?" she asked to loosen him up. Lynn figured he wasn't too bright by the way he was babbling on the way to the precinct. Maybe she could get him to trip up and talk about Muldoon. Mosh looked at Lynn and said he was all right. "This questioning is being video recorded, that okay?" Mosh just nodded.

"Did you really think you were going to blow up the house with people in it?"

"I had no plans of blowing anything up; I found the bag on the ground and was bringing it to the house to see if they lost it."

Lynn sat just staring at Mosh, not believing what she was hearing. "Mosh, I'm sure when forensics gets done with examining the bag, they will find your prints all over the detonator and the dynamite. What do you think about that?"

He was quiet. "Well, uh, when I found the bag on the road, I did take the stuff out of the bag, to, you know, check it. Maybe my prints got there from that."

"You weren't worried that it might have blown up, killing you?"

"Nah, the timer wasn't set yet?"

"How did you know that?"

"Uh, I could see the timer wasn't set."

"Strange, Forensics said there was no timer on the dynamite, it was set-up to blow by a phone call, which strangely enough was going to come from your cell phone. How about that?"

"Wow, someone had my phone number?"

Lynn just sat staring at him, "Do you think we are so stupid to believe you?"

"I hope so; I don't really want to be put in a cell with Willis. He's crazy."

Bob Moats

Lynn's chest was shaking from stifling a laugh. "Mosh, aren't you worried what your uncle Muldoon may do to you if we release you?"

"Are you going to release me?" He said happily.

"No, Mosh, we are not going to release you, we have you dead on for the murder of Brantley, pardon the pun. So you and Willis can do a tango together in prison. What did Uncle Muldoon want you to do with the dynamite, Mosh?"

"Hunh? I didn't do anything for Uncle Muldoon. It was my idea not his, I do think on my own you know." He seemed annoyed.

Lynn played up on that, "Well, Muldoon made most of the decisions, didn't he? So you say you were going to show him that you can handle things yourself?"

"Yeah, he wanted that bitch to be out of the picture and he sent Willis to handle it but he got caught. I decided to show Uncle that I could handle it." He said proudly.

"Where did you get the dynamite, why not C4?"

"Easier to get dynamite, I broke into a construction company over where they are building that new casino. They had it in a cabinet, it was locked but I got in."

Sin City Murders

"You said Uncle Muldoon wanted the bitch taken care of, is this the girl who saw you and Willis murder Brantley?"

"Yeah, she was going to blow the whole thing, without her around the case was going to be weak. At least that's what Uncle Muldoon said. Hey, I'm not saying anything more without my lawyer. I deny everything I said."

"A little too late for that, Mosh. Thank you for your cooperation and we'll tell Uncle Muldoon that you were very chatty about the murder of Brantley and the attempt on the life of Lacey Lee. Hope he can't get to you."

Mosh was looking real frightened now, "Hey I need protection, I have to have protection. You got an obligation to protect me."

"Protect you from what Mosh, from Uncle Muldoon?"

"Oh, you don't know what he can do! He has people in his pocket, important people, and dangerous people. He has people above him running the whole Sin City project who don't want things screwed up. They wouldn't like it. Even Uncle Muldoon is afraid of them."

**

Chapter 22

"Sin City project? What's that Mosh?"

"I'm not saying anything more to you; I'm in deep enough now. I want my lawyer."

Lynn stood and looked to the mirror and shrugged. She turned to the cop waiting to take Mosh to his cell and said, "Put him in with Willis, so they can talk about the bad things they did."

Mosh looked shocked, "Hey! I don't want to be anywhere near Willis. You can't put me in his cell cause you know what he'll do."

"Mosh, you wanted your lawyer, so we can't talk anymore. You'll just have to wait in your cell until your lawyer gets here."

"Okay, let's not be hasty about this. Why don't we just sit and talk some more, maybe we can come to some understanding that would benefit us all?"

Lynn could see he was sweating now; she turned to him and smiled. "All right Mosh, let's talk. Sit and relax, we have time. Would you like a drink, water, soda pop or something, other than alcohol?" She smiled.

"Yeah, that would be nice, you have cola?" Lynn looked to the cop and asked if he could get a cola for Mosh, he went out.

"Now what do you want to talk about Mosh? Let's start with what this Sin City project you mentioned is?"

He sat nervously looking around and then cleared his throat, "Am I gonna be protected now, before I spill anything?"

"I'll see if we can make a nice deal with the DA for your testimony."

"You gotta promise me first."

"I'll make promises if your info is good Mosh, otherwise forget it."

"Okay, I'll trust you. The Sin City project is a group of wealthy men who want to be wealthier. They are going to build the biggest whore house and gambling casino in Vegas once the prostitution bill is passed. Right in the middle of town, they already have the property and the building is going up, just needs the right people to fill it, you know hookers and johns."

"Are you talking about the Merkins casino project on Sahara, where the vacant lot used to be?"

"Yeah, that's the place. This guy Merkins has a lot of backers who have their hands into strip clubs and illegal gambling operations around the country. They want to consolidate their holdings into one big fucking palace of porn. Gambling along with stores that sell sex toys and DVD's, massage parlors and of course the hookers in private rooms. All in one place, a pervert's dream. They even plan a convention center so the porn video awards convention can be held there. The whole place will attract horny men like flies to garbage." He sat back grinning. The cop brought back a cola for Mosh in a paper cup. He thanked the cop and continued, "Merkins knew my Uncle Muldoon had councilmen on his blackmail list so he got Uncle to get on the council by getting rid of Brantley so the bill would pass. He set it up to look like a flagrante delicto with a hooker gone bad. Except the woman that Paul Martinez brought in messed up the scheme by disappearing before Mason could get the investigation in motion. Martinez had to go grab a hooker from downtown to fill in. Willis was the one who stabbed both Brantley and the girl, I just watched, I can't kill anyone."

"Except with dynamite." Lynn threw the comment in.

"Okay, I was trying to redeem myself with Uncle. I stood out front of that house and wasn't even sure if I could do it. I ain't no killer. If that big guy hadn't snuck up behind me and coldcocked me, I might have just walked away." He looked to the floor and went silent.

"Who killed Martinez?"

"Willis, bullet to the back of the head. Willis said he was a liability. I was worried Willis would think I was a liability, but that would piss off Uncle Muldoon if he killed me."

"Muldoon must have some documentation of blackmail on the councilmen, do you know where or how he keeps it?"

"He has this big safe in his strip club, in the basement. That's where he keeps everything."

Lynn turned to the cop again and said, "Take our Mr. Mosh to a nice quiet cell, away from Willis." The cop grinned and took Mosh out; Lynn came into the observation room and leaned against the wall.

"Well Lacey, is the mystery coming together for you?"

Lacey looked upset having to go through this, but she picked her chin up and said, "I think I'll sleep better now."

"No more suicide attempts either?"

"No, I've had my fill of trying to kill myself. Now that I know why I thought I was crazy, it's all good now."

Penny said, "You're not out of the woods yet, there are still bad people out there who don't want you testifying in court, I'm sure."

Lynn agreed, "Yes, there are going to be a few more people to put away before you can totally relax. But we'll keep an eye on you so don't worry."

I was just standing on the side taking it all in. I knew the police were getting close now to nabbing the people involved in Brantley's murder plot and putting Muldoon into office. I could now tell Mrs. Brantley what happened and her husband wasn't in on any sex play with hookers.

I looked at my watch; it was just now before noon, so I asked, "Lynn, are we done here? I'd like to get back to the office to finish a few things."

"I don't see anything we'd need you for, but thank you for all the help you, Penny and Lacey have given."

"Don't forget Buck, he caught Mosh." I smiled.

"Tell him we owe him too."

We left the observation room and I took Penny and Lacey out to the car. Willy was just about going through the windows as we arrived and he sat in back with Lacey, looking pissed at us. "Our son is not pleased with us; we need to take him with us more often."

"Okay, you wear the purse then." Penny laughed. Lacey knew what we were talking about and said, "I'll carry Willy in his doggy carrier if you don't mind."

I looked to Penny and said, "We have a doggy nanny now. Hand her the purse." Penny laughed and picked up the carrier from the floor by her feet and handed it to Lacey.

I asked if anyone was hungry and took everybody to Carl's Jr. for food.

~~*~~

Buck took Mac and two of his biggest guards out to the office of Retcho Security. Mac and the two guards had at one time worked for Retcho; they were going to enjoy this visit. They pulled up to the office building and went into the lobby with Buck asking the receptionist if they could see John Retcho Sr. about a personal matter. She recognized Mac and asked how he was doing.

"Much better since I left here. Is John Sr. in?"

"Yes he is, I'll let him know you want to see him," she said as she looked to Buck and picked up the phone. "Mr. Retcho, there are some gentlemen here to see you about a personal matter." She paused, "I'll send them in."

She looked to Mac, smiled and said, "You know where the office is."

"Yep, thanks Connie, good to see you again." Mac led the men down a hall to an office, knocked and when he heard Retcho say to come in, he opened the door and let Buck go first.

Buck came up to Retcho's desk followed by his men as Retcho looked surprised by seeing the three former guards. "May I help you?" he asked.

Buck leaned over, putting his knuckles on the desk and grumbled, "I don't take kindly to threats, and least of all childish vandalism on property my men are guarding."

Retcho sat back and said, "I presume you are with Richards Investigations and Security?"

"Now what makes you think that, you know me somehow? You know about threats made to my office? You know about someone shooting an air rifle at the cars your guards used to guard?"

"Nope, I know nothing about your accusations." He gave a big grin to Buck and just stared.

Buck pulled a digital voice recorder out of his pocket and turned it on. The recorder played the threat made on the phone and then Buck played the call made from the call back and someone answered saying that it was Retcho's office.

"What's that prove?" He was not grinning now.

"I've been asked to take this recording to the cops and maybe they can pull a voice match from it. Just be aware that from now on we will fire on anyone firing on us, air guns or real guns, you have been warned." Buck put the recorder back in his pocket stood up straight and signaled his men to leave, he turned at the door and said, "I'm not here to fight with you, there's plenty of jobs out there for guards, just stay in your own backyard and we'll get along." He went out.

~~*~~

We were sitting in Carl's Jr. enjoying our burgers and fries, when my phone rang. Caller ID said it was Lynn, "Hello super cop. What's up now?"

"Jim, Willis is dead and Mosh is barely holding on. We got him to the infirmary in time to save him, they were slipped a poison. We're going over the logs of every fucking person who had access to them, but it's looking bleak. Keep a close eye on Lacey or maybe we should put her in a safe house. I don't want to see your new home blown up. Be careful."

I hung up and looked to my girls, and thought it was time to get out of town. Maybe a nice camping trip to the mountains.

Chapter 23

Lynn had her warrant for Muldoon and a search warrant for the strip club to search for the safe. She knew they'd have to move fast before Muldoon moved the evidence, so she sent a team of cops led by Detective Warren to the club first while she took another team to Muldoon's office. Deacon had warned her what to expect when she saw Muldoon. Lynn and her men moved into Muldoon's office at City Hall startling a good number of political employees. They walked right past the secretary as she was asking what they wanted, standing looking surprised. Lynn said to one of the men to watch the secretary so they could take her in for questioning about Muldoon's activities, then she turned to Muldoon's door and went in without knocking.

Lynn was shocked at the sight of the enormously huge man, but more surprised at the purple condition of his face and his tongue hanging out the side of his mouth. Lynn ran to him and checked his pulse but couldn't be sure if she could find it under the mounds of fat. She put her ear close to his mouth and heard nothing, no breathing. She told one of her men to call EMT and the ME to check the body and they would also need him to run tests immediately for poisons. She picked up a cup of what looked like cola and smelled it, no outstanding odors to suggest the drink had been poisoned, but it would be easy enough to slip some unknown poison into it.

Lynn went back out to the lobby and found the secretary was still there and came to her. "Who brought the drink to Muldoon?"

"I did, I got it from the machine down the hall."

"Were there any visitors to Muldoon in the last hour or two?"

"Sure, he had a number of visitors; I can get you a list."

"Do that now, thanks." Lynn looked to Deacon, "I feel sorry for the coroner taking him out of the office."

Deacon smiled and said "I told you they would need a forklift."

About a half hour later she could hear Joseph Lang, the medical examiner, cursing to beat hell. He came out of Muldoon's office and said he needed some more help and a larger gurney or two tied together. He stood looking back through the door and said, "How can someone live like that. His internal organs must be a mess. He's going to be a challenge to autopsy, but I love a challenge. Oh and just a preliminary COD, by the condition of his skin and mouth, I'd say it's a good bet that he was poisoned, but I'll know better once I have him into the morgue." He pulled his cell phone and walked back into the office.

Lynn got a call from Detective Warren at the strip club and was told they had the safe and were waiting for the locksmith to open it. They were gathering everything they could from the office in the club, maybe they'd find something there that would help. Lynn told him about Muldoon's murder and she could hear him curse softly on the other end.

Warren said, "Someone didn't want him and his boys talking. Good that we got a statement from Mosh, now we just have to hope he lives to testify." He signed off and Lynn watched four big cops walk in pulling two gurneys handcuffed together. They took it into the office and about a half hour later, struggling, pushing and pulling they managed to get him on the gurneys. They covered him and wheeled him out to the elevator which they worried wouldn't hold up under his weight. A custodian saw them and suggested they use the service elevator. They thanked him and he escorted them there.

"Okay, Muldoon and Willis are dead and Mosh is barely alive. There's not much more for Lacey to testify about or worry about. I don't think Merkins gives a crap about small fish, especially since they are all dead and so far we have no physical evidence connecting him to Muldoon. We should let it be known that Mosh is also dead and keep him under wraps. He may be more interested in talking now that he knows what they think of him."

Lynn went out to the hallway to call me and I was relieved that Lacey was better off now. I still thought it would be a good idea to get out of the city for a couple of days and told her of my intentions. She laughed and said to remember to take my cell phone in case a cougar attacks. I said, "The only cougar I worry about is Penny." I stifled a laugh as she whacked my arm and stuck her tongue out.

"I'm puzzled about something though. If Merkins needed Muldoon's vote to pass the bill why kill him?" I asked.

"Good question. Something may come up in the stuff we gather at the strip club. Enjoy your camping and I'll keep you informed." I thanked her and we disconnected the call.

I told Penny and Lacey about what was going on and Lacey took a sigh of relief. Penny asked where we were going camping, I told her up on Mt. Charleston. "There's a small campground up there but we need to go to Wal-Marts for some extra supplies." We drove over to the store and I told Penny to grab an extra cart; Lacey carried Willy in his purse. We went straight to the sporting goods section and I grabbed a number of things I knew from experience that we would need. I saw a real nice three room tent with privacy flaps and it was on sale, I liked that, so bought it. I knew the tent we already had was too small for all of us. The only bad part of having everyone in the same tent was privacy. No good sex unless we could be very, very quiet. I knew we couldn't.

We packed everything in the car and drove to the office, where we found Buck and his men having a meeting. He saw us come in and came over.

"How'd it go with Retcho?" I asked.

"Well, he understands my position on the matter. I'm warning my men to shoot first, question later." He grinned.

"I hope it doesn't come to that, our insurance man may not like it." I told him all that happened today and that I was taking the women camping for a couple days just to unwind.

"I like that. Maybe someday I'll drag Maria with us and we can all go."

"Have you ever camped?" I asked.

"Hell yes, I'm an old biker remember? I've had to camp out many times while riding out in the world." He grinned with that walrus smile.

"True, now you can run the office while I'm gone. No murder cases for a while, we've had enough this last week."

Buck laughed and went back to his meeting with his men. They finished up a bit later and his men all headed out as Penny and I sat talking about the camping trip. Lacey was out at the reception desk playing with Willy when two men came in the front entrance and asked Lacey if they could talk to Jim Richards. I had heard what was said and came out to meet them.

"I'm Jim Richards, may I help you."

They pulled badges identifying themselves as agents of the ATF; I wondered what they wanted with me. "We are investigating the Merkins casino project and need to take Lacey Lee in for questioning. Is she here?" They evidently didn't know who Lacey was.

I called Buck and he came out, I said these men want to take Lacey with them. He stood behind me with his hand on his .38 and smiled at the men.

"Gentlemen, I would have to call Detective Lieutenant Lynn Carter, Metro police before I even think about letting Miss Lee go anywhere, if she were here." Lacey was sitting quietly with Willy now and I could tell she wasn't going to say anything.

"Do you know where Miss Lee is at the moment?" one agent asked.

"I have an idea of where she is, but again, Lieutenant Carter would have to be apprised of the situation." I asked Penny, standing behind me, to call Lynn, she went to my office. "Now explain what your interest is with Miss Lee?"

"That's our business and it is part of an investigation of corruption in the gaming industry. Please have Miss Lee come in to talk." He looked to Lacey still sitting quietly and I walked to the counter and said to Lacey, "Mildred, would you call Lacey and see what she's doing." Lacey picked up on my cue and took the phone and pretended to call. I knew that the Nevada State Gaming Board were the people who would take on illegal operations in gambling, not ATF.

The men started to get antsy and I asked if they could please have a seat until Miss Lee arrived, hoping Lynn got here soon. I went to the counter again and said, "Mildred, would you please take Willy to the back room and feed him, I'm sure he's hungry." She nodded and took the dog from the desk and went down the hall to the back. Buck was still standing behind me and I winked at him. Penny stuck her head out the office door and said Lynn was on her way, with Deacon. I said good and turned to see two patrol cars come flying up to the building and the police all streamed out of the cars coming to the entrance.

I had my Glock in my hand now and Buck had drawn his .38, I held my gun up and asked the men to just put their hands up in the air as the police were coming in. The men looked shocked and raised their hands high. The first cop was familiar to me and I said, 'Hey Ted, we need to check on our friends here to see if they are legit as ATF agents."

He went to the men and asked for ID, they hesitated and Ted asked them to stand. The first man was just starting to stand as he tried to draw his gun, I fired on him hitting his shoulder and he spun to the ground as the other man just sat, not moving. Ted frisked him and pulled out a .45 from his belt. One of the other cops called for an EMS and then called Lynn. He said she was on her way, and explained that she had called them after Penny called her, to come by since they were in the area to protect us. Ted and his men had the phony ATF men handcuffed and ready by the time Lynn and Deacon came flying up. Medical techs who arrived just before Lynn, were bandaging the wound on the arm of the first man and said it was superficial.

"You just can't stay out of trouble can you?" she said smiling at me. She went to the first man and called for Ted to bring in the fingerprint ID scanner. I remembered when Earl Daws had one of the scanners during the movie murders back in Detroit. It was a device that can scan a finger and send the print info back to the lab for ID. They checked each of the men and after a short while the device came back with identification of the men as felons and wanted by the Feds.

Lynn looked to me and said, "They're bad boys."

**

Chapter 24

"After we're done with them, I may turn them over to the FBI for impersonating Federal Agents. Besides they're wanted by the Feds, so it's less we have to worry about." Lynn said.

"This proves one thing; someone still wants Lacey out of the picture." Deacon spoke now.

"Yeah, I was thinking that too. Maybe Merkins knows about the mess that Muldoon and his gang started and he's trying to clean it up. What happened with the safe?" I asked.

"Oh, yeah, it was empty. Not a scrap of paper to be found. Either Mosh was wrong about the safe containing the blackmail evidence or someone got to it before killing Muldoon. Warren is questioning the employees of the strip club to see who may have been in the safe recently." Lynn turned to watch the two men being led out by the cops. "We keep piling up suspects but nothing to link to Merkins."

"Maybe Merkins sent someone to empty the safe so they could kill Muldoon and still blackmail the councilmen." I offered.

"Either way I think there will be a slowing down on the issue; the bill doesn't come up to vote until next week Friday. We have six days to get this worked out. If Merkins has the goods on the councilmen, time will tell, and with Brantley out of the picture being the big objector of the bill, it stands a better chance to pass. Even without Muldoon."

"Well I have a camping trip to organize, we'll be gone till Wednesday, you won't need us until then will you?" I asked.

"We won't need you at all hopefully. Lacey can only testify about the murder of Brantley by Mosh and Willis, but with Willis dead and Mosh not able to talk for now, there's not much of a case. So go enjoy your trip, I know you've been wanting to play nature boy since you got here." Lynn laughed.

"Just don't freeze up there, it's still winter and you're going to be over a mile up. It's damn cold up there." Deacon offered.

"I'll just turn on my portable heater." I said as I looked to Penny. She smiled and said, "I'm not going to be much warmth for you, that's why you bought the tent heater."

"And extra blankets." I added.

Lynn looked to Lacey sitting back again at the desk with Willy, "Have you even asked Lacey if she wanted to go camping? Maybe she's not the outdoors type."

I turned to Lacey and asked her again, "Lacey, are you good to go camping?"

"I love camping, besides I couldn't leave Willy out there to get eaten by a bear now could I?"

"Bear?" Penny looked to me, "You didn't say anything about bears?"

Deacon laughed and said, "There are no bears up there, maybe a mountain lion, but no bears."

"Mountain lions? Not good either," she said.

"Hey, you're armed now, use it." I said.

"Believe it, and don't go wandering outside the tent at night, I may shoot." She gave me a cute little smirk. I kissed her cheek and said, "You'd miss me." She replied, "Not with the gun."

Everyone had left the office and I could see that Lynn was out in the parking lot talking to Deacon. He would look over to the office every so often as they talked. He was grinning and then he kissed her on the cheek, she went to the car as Deacon came back into the office.

"What are you two cooking up out there?" I asked.

"Lynn says I'm getting grumpy lately so she is telling me to go camping. You guys have room for me and my tent?"

I laughed and said, "We'd be more than happy to have you along."

"Well, it was that, or I go back to processing gangbangers. Guess what I'm going to do?"

"Have you ever camped before?"

"Oh, hell yeah, I camped a lot back in Desert Storm and also in field exercises at the police academy."

"I didn't know you were in Desert Storm?"

"Something I'd rather not talk about, if you don't mind."

"Nope, I don't mind at all. So you have your own equipment?"

"Yep, I'll run home and gather it up and meet you back here. What time?"

"I'll call you, we have to go home and I have to convince Penny not to pack ten suitcases."

He laughed and said he'd wait for our call, then went out to the car where Lynn waited.

Penny said, "Looks like we have a bodyguard. Oh, and I resent that crack about packing ten suitcases."

"Well, can you refrain from taking more clothes than you'll need for three days in the wild?"

"I can and you'll see." She smiled and walked into my office to get her purse. We left after I told Buck that we would be back Wednesday, but if he had any problems to call me.

We spent the next hour getting our gear ready to go and I was surprised that Penny came out with only two suitcases. She smiled pleasantly and went to help Lacey get ready. We had everything in the car and headed back to the office after I called Deacon to say we were ready to go.

We met him in the parking lot and Lynn drove over in her car to see us off. Deacon was taking his monster Chevy pickup truck so he had a good number of camping items in the bed of the huge truck. I was looking at what he was bringing, tent, folding camp tables, larger cooler which I hoped was stocked with beer and then I saw the generator up front of the bed. "Well it's good that we'll have power to recharge our cell phones." I joked.

"Never know when we'll need power to watch TV." He grinned and lifted a tarp to show the small portable color TV.

"Don't let Penny see that before we leave." I said.

Lynn gave Deacon a kiss good-bye and we went off toward the mountain. I could see the thing ahead of us and remembered when my son and I drove up this road the last time I lived here. I also remembered why we didn't get to the top, I was low on gas, and there are no gas stations on the mountain. So this time I was sure I had checked my gas gauge and had a full tank. As we drove the road upwards, Penny was reading the elevation signs to remind us how high we were going.

"We just passed the 5000 foot elevation; we've gone up 2000 feet since the last sign." Penny was playing our tour guide, I could see the signs but she enjoyed announcing our altitude at every sign we passed. We passed into the Spring Mountains National Recreation area and I checked my mirror to be sure Deacon was still back there, he was.

We went up another half mile and eventually came up to where the Old Mill campground was located. Penny announced that we were at 8300 feet elevation, over a mile and a half above sea level. It was nice and woodsy and had a small stream running along the road. We crossed over a wooden bridge after we parked along the road. There was a small building that was sort of a tourist information center and we had to go in to register. There were only two other campers that I could see, so we had the place pretty much to ourselves.

I had Penny help set our new tent up so she knew what to do in case I was unable to set the thing up. Deacon had his tent up in record time and was getting the fire pit ready with whatever wood he could find for kindling. He went to the building where he was able to buy bundles of firewood and came back with two bundles.

It was starting to get dark now, not totally, but close. The sun was still up at our altitude and I was sure if we could see the valley it would be a lot darker. We pulled out the folding chairs that I bought and Deacon got the fire going nicely. It was starting to chill a bit so we all put on warmer clothes, I could hear Penny grumble about the weather and how she would stay home next time. Willy was tethered to a long leash; we didn't want him taking off into the woods like he would do back in Michigan on our property. He was happy rolling in the dirt so we let him enjoy himself.

Sin City Murders

It was dark out now and our only light at the moment was the campfire. Deacon was sitting next to me and we all had our beers in hand. Lacey had Pepsi since she didn't like alcohol, mostly from having a father who over indulged in the spirits.

"I used to love camping out years back, although I didn't like camping in the middle of a war." Deacon spoke. "I spent eighteen months in support for the grunts who went into the villages and were lucky to come back out." He went silent; I wasn't going to ask him about it, he would tell me if he wanted to. "This world sucks; I see it every day as a cop. But then there are the people who thank us for helping them and occasionally catching the bad guys. It balances out sometimes. This trip is what I have needed for a while, especially to get away from the damn gangbangers. Boy, they frost my ass." He laughed out loud, it sounded good to me.

I turned to the right when I heard a car driving up and suddenly a spotlight flicked on, bathing us in bright light. I had my hand on my Glock waiting for the worst, Deacon was on his feet. Suddenly we heard a P.A. quietly blare, "Don't even think about pulling those guns." The voice came forth from the car speakers, it was Lynn.

**

Chapter 25

I turned on the camp lantern so we could see better as Lynn opened the passenger door of the LVMPD patrol car and got out. She opened the back door and took out a small suitcase.

"Look out Deacon, she's moving in," I said. I could see Lynn present me her middle finger and Deacon laughed. She came around to the driver and said something to him, he nodded, smiled, and yelled to Deacon, "Hurry back, the gangs have been asking for you." He drove off and turned the car around further up and then went back down the road.

"What are you doing here?" Deacon asked.

"I figured you'd need protection and Weber told me to get out of town for a day or two while he did some checking around about Merkins. He said he'd call if he needed us. I think he is being pressured by accounting for all the overtime the department has run up so far on this case." She looked to me.

"Hey, don't blame me for the extra expenses." I defended.

Sin City Murders

Penny was happy to see Lynn and the three women went into a huddle, gossiping. Deacon and I went back to sitting with our beer and watched the fire eventually burn down as we were out of wood, so we all decided to turn in. Lynn had put her gear into Deacon's tent and Lacey took Willy into her section of the big tent after saying good night. Penny and I went into our room and she was into the sleeping bag in record time. I took my time getting in and I whispered, "Think if we could be real quiet we could have a little sex." She laughed and said 'Hell, no. You'll just have to wait till we come up by ourselves, then we'll only frighten the mountain lions."

Penny was asleep quickly as always and I just lay there listening to the noises of the woods. I could hear snoring coming from Deacon's general direction, at least I hoped it was Deacon and not Lynn. I unzipped the window cover on the side of the tent so I could look out at the sky facing the mountain. I could see the beam of light in the distance coming from the Luxor Hotel pyramid wondering at its power. We were about thirty-five miles from Vegas but the light shone brightly.

I guess I had finally fallen asleep, because Penny was shaking me to get up. The sun was peeking up over the mountain behind us, it was still a little dark in the woods, but light enough to see that the women had put the cooking gear together and had made breakfast. Lynn was still dragging Deacon out of his coma; I stepped out of our tent and took a big deep breath. It was good, cold but good.

We had our breakfast and since it was Sunday, Deacon figured there was probably a football game on. Lynn said, "If you so much as turn that generator on for the TV, I swear I'll marry you just to divorce you."

We sat around the campground just relaxing and talking. Lynn spoke, "Weber said without Muldoon and Willis and with Mosh still in critical condition, there's not much can be done right now. We still have to come up with some evidence of blackmail against the councilmen to even get a warrant for Merkins. Weber is going to nose around with his connections to see what they can come up with."

So the world comes to a screeching halt as crime goes on." Penny said.

"That's about it; the wheels of justice turn slowly in real life. But Merkins will screw up somewhere along the way." Lynn offered.

"So with Muldoon out of the picture, Merkins will have to really put pressure on the remaining councilmen to pass the bill. Did you ever find out what killed Muldoon?" I asked.

Lynn smiled and said, "The ME hasn't gotten the tox report back yet but figures he was given a combination of drugs that gave him a reaction, his throat closed up and he strangled to death. He was so fat he couldn't get up to save himself. Justice has been served."

"What about Mason?" I asked.

"He's under protective custody and giving his statement, he really knows very little about the operation, other than what Muldoon wanted him to know. Anything he says may help, but for now he's being put on the back burner."

My cell phone rang and the caller ID said unknown. I didn't like those calls, but answered. "Hello, this better not be a sales pitch." I said.

It was Buck. "Jimmy, I need your help man, I'm in jail."

I sat up and said, "What? Why?"

"I supposedly beat up on John Retcho Sr.; at least that's what the cops say. They have been real nice to me, but I'd like to get out of here."

"Where are you at?"

"Lynn and Deacon's precinct. That's why they are being nice to me. But I still want to get out; I'm having bad flashes from my past."

194

"Okay, hang tight, I'm up in the mountains so it will be a short while, but I'll be there." I hung up and looked to Deacon and Lynn, "Buck's in your jail, for attacking Retcho Sr. or so they say."

Deacon looked stunned, "Buck? Oh hell no, I've known him long enough to know he wouldn't attack someone, he'd defend himself but not attack." He looked to Lynn and said, "I'm going down with Jim to see what this is all about."

Lynn said to go and call if he needed her. Penny looked concerned and I told her it'd be all right, I'll get Buck out of jail and get to the bottom of this. I asked the women if they would be all right, Lynn laughed, "There are two women here with guns who know how to shoot, we'll be all right. Now go break Buck out of jail."

Deacon and I got in my car and we drove down the mountain arriving at Metro precinct about forty minutes later. We parked and went in the back way straight to the holding cells. Deacon was able to get us into the cell block and we found Buck sitting on the hard bench looking hot.

"Okay prisoner, what happened?" I joked.

"I was in the office minding my own business and these two cops came in and said they had a warrant for my arrest. One of the cops was that Ted guy so I knew he wasn't joking. Retcho said I came to him in his parking lot and attacked him, his weasel of a son said he saw it all. Mother fuckers, I'll show them what attacking is when I get out of here."

"You're going to do no such thing. Deacon explained to me you'll have to get bail posted before they let you out and the judge won't be in until tomorrow, today is Sunday."

"Shit, I have to stay in here over night!" He roared.

"I'll go talk to Retcho to see what this is about. Give me some time and I'll try and get you out." I told him to hang in as Deacon and I left.

"I have an idea, you'll need to help, let's go over to visit Retcho." I said.

"You're not going to shoot him are you?"

"No, I'd like to, but I may need you to cover my back. You'll see."

We went back out to my car and drove over to the address I had of Retcho Security. We parked and went to the door, it was locked but there was a man in a guard uniform inside at the counter. I knocked and the guard came over and opened the door.

"Is John Retcho in?" I asked. He asked if we wanted Junior or Senior. I said Senior, the guard said he was and let us in. He pointed to a door down the hall and said he had to go to his job site then left.

We walked to the door, it was open and a man sat at the desk going through some papers. We walked in and he was surprised to see us.

"Your guards don't seem to be doing their jobs." I said. "I could be here to kill you, but they just let us waltz in unannounced. Pretty crappy operations you got here."

"Who the hell are you?" He asked.

I walked to his desk and said, "Jim Richards, you seemed to have a problem with my partner, Buck Carson."

"That animal attacked me!" He said loudly, but there was no one to hear him, the office was empty now.

"Don't play that on me you scum. Buck would never attack anyone and if he did attack you, you would be in the hospital. I don't see any serious bruises on you. You made this whole thing up didn't you, you pus boil you."

"Screw you! I'll see that jerk get what's coming to him."

"You can't even hold on to simple jobs of guarding car lots can you? How do you even keep this company going, you don't have any sense of what you're doing do you? Buck takes one of your clients and you act like a baby by shooting windshields and setting up people with false complaints. You're a mental case aren't you."

He stood now coming around the desk, "Who the hell do you think you are, coming in here and telling me how to run my business? I'll call the cops and have you put away for trespass."

"Whoa, tough man, eh, asswipe. You think you can stop me from saying what I want? I don't intimidate easily, pervert. Speaking of perverts, where's that mealy mouth son of yours?"

He finally went off and grabbed my throat with his left hand and took a swing at my head with his right. I turned just in time to keep my nose from making contact with his fist, then he started to take a swing again and Deacon grabbed his arm, twisting it behind his back. He let go of my neck and was howling.

"Sir, I'm a police officer, you are under arrest for assault with intent to do bodily harm." Deacon said as Retcho kicked him in the leg. "Oh and resisting arrest and striking a police officer. Not looking good for you."

Deacon had Retcho's hands cuffed and was pulling him out of the office reading his rights, as he cursed and yelled.

In the lobby, I got my face close to his and said, 'Gee, the judge won't be in until tomorrow to post bail, you'll have to spend the night in lockup. You and Buck can share a cell."

**

Chapter 26

Retcho was looking rather timid now while he sat handcuffed on a chair in his lobby, as Deacon was calling for a car to pick him up. I sat down next to him, "You know this can all go away very easily, just drop charges against Buck and you can go free also. I mean we both know your charges on Buck were fabricated. Otherwise you'll be doing some time alongside a very mean man who will make your life miserable. Won't do your business very much good either for an owner to be imprisoned on all of these charges. You could lose your license. So what do you say?"

He gave me a stare with bloodshot eyes, heavy drinking I figured, usually ruptures the blood vessels in the eyes and nose. He looked to the window and was biting his lower lip, thinking I guessed. "If I drop charges then you won't arrest me?"

"Nope, it all goes away, unless you back out of it, so we may have to take you in for booking then I'll drop charges after you get Buck released, just to be sure. Besides, this gentleman is a homicide detective; it's his word against yours. Who do you think the police will believe?"

"Shit. Okay, I'll drop charges," he said reluctantly. I turned to Deacon and he was grinning as he got back on his cell phone and called a buddy of his at the precinct to say that the charges were being dropped on Buck. Retcho would still have to go in to sign off on the complaint, so we waited till the patrol car came and Deacon said to take good care of our prisoner. We drove after the patrol car and went in to see Buck being processed out. Retcho was signing some papers and looking miserable, I told Buck to leave him alone now. Deacon released Retcho and I gave him a five for a cab back to his office. He stormed out of the station and we stood watching him go.

"I hope this is going to be the end of it. I don't think my face can take another punch." I laughed.

Buck looked at the mild bruise on the side of my face and said, "You did that for me? You are a sweetheart." Then he grabbed my head and gave me a big kiss on the cheek. I pulled away and said to back off or I'll have him arrested for assault.

We went out to my car, Deacon and I drove Buck back to the office. On the way back up the mountain, we joked about the stunt I pulled at Retcho's office. Deacon said, "I figured you were trying to get his anger up, so I just waited for him to move on you, giving him enough time to hit you."

"Well, I didn't know if he had a short fuse but it worked." We finally drove into to the campground again and we couldn't see any of the women at the campsite. I was worried. We parked and went over, I found a note on the camp table saying they took a hike on the trail and would be back soon. Deacon liked that and pulled the generator out of the truck bed and set it up. He cranked it over, surprisingly it was rather quiet. He pulled the TV out and set it on the table plugging it in and turned it to the first football game he could find. I didn't like sports so I told him I was going over to the visitor information center to look over their brochures. He nodded and I walked away.

I was going through the racks of brochures so I would have more things to do while living in Vegas. May as well take advantage of all the fun. About a half hour later I went back to the campsite and found Deacon sitting on the chaise lounge and the women were watching a cooking show on one of the local stations. I had to laugh quietly so not to offend Deacon, but he looked so miserable on the chair.

Penny saw me and came bouncing over, latching on to me with a big wet kiss. "I hear you saved Buck's bacon," she said.

"Well, I did what I would do for any friend." I smiled and then made a face, the bruise hurt a bit. Penny saw it and kissed it carefully.

"You're my hero," she spoke then pulled me to the picnic table and sat me down. "I need to talk to you about something. While you were gone saving Buck I got a call from Gordy back in Michigan. It seems he has been in touch with a couple of his friends here in Vegas who are managers at KLAS TV and told them I was out of my contract with the station. His friends were excited and wanted to talk to me about taking on a daily talk show here in Vegas." She stopped talking and waited for me to speak.

"Wow, that's something you've talked about for a while now. All the glitz and glamour of having your own show here, with all the celebrities for your picking. So what do you think?"

"I think I need to talk to the people here to see what they expect and what they offer. I'll need lots of money for this, so you can live the lifestyle you are becoming accustom to." She grinned and kissed my cheek again.

"Well, go talk, when do they want to see you?"

"Monday."

"That's tomorrow."

"I know, but it's so cold camping now, we can come back in the summer and do this again."

I sat giving her my most harsh look, then cracked a smile and said, "Okay by me, I'll never deny you anything you want, except a divorce. I may put my foot down to that. But you know this will end your career as a private investigator."

"Sorry sweetie, but I gots ta do what I gots ta do," she said. I laughed and asked what time her meeting was. "Anytime I say, they are going to cater to my whims." She gave me that evil little smile I grew to love.

"Does Lynn and Lacey know about this?"

"Yes, we were out on the trail when Gordy called, then some bigwig named Kent Reser from KLAS called about the meeting. I told them I'd think about it and call them with a time."

"Call him back and set it up. But later in the afternoon so we can spend one more night in the cold."

She hugged me then pulled her phone out and made the call. I sat listening to her being stroked by her future employers. I hoped she really wants this.

We spent the rest of the day playing campers and enjoying the warmth that suddenly moved in. We got more wood that night and had a big campfire and even roasted marshmallows. I was quite tired by midnight and said we had to pull up stakes in the morning to go make Penny a star. We all headed to our sleeping bags and I actually slept well.

Next morning we woke early and started tearing down the camp. I made sure we left it the way we found it. Deacon and Lynn said they were heading back to the precinct to see what came up with the two fake feds. Lynn turned them over to Warren and he was going to question them. They left, Penny and Lacey got into the car and we headed home.

I told Penny that I would unpack the car and she could go get ready for her interview. Lacey asked if she could use the pool and I told her that would be fine with me and said to take Willy with her. She went off and I finally finished putting everything away, figuring we wouldn't be camping again for a long time, if at all. Well, it was fun while it lasted, but our lives usually seemed just too busy or hectic for relaxing.

Penny came out thirty minutes later looking great in a short skirt, blue silk blouse and spike heels. She always knew how to dress for business meetings. I decided to leave Lacey here while we were gone so I called her in the house to show her a few things she needed to know while we were out. I showed her the security panel and how it worked, then took her to our best feature of the house, in case of attack by marauding bandits, our panic room. It was in the master bedroom and I showed her how to open, close and lock the door if she needed to avoid capture. I showed her the cell phone that was in the room for calls out, in case the house phone lines were cut. I also showed her the pump action shotgun, loaded by the door, just in case. She was impressed and I felt confident enough to leave her alone.

I told her to be careful in the pool and we left, heading to KLAS. I had been in the station one other time when I worked for Nick North, when he was on a morning talk show talking about his act at the Flamingo Hotel. We pulled in and parked by the main entrance, Penny said she was nervous.

"You've done your show for over five years, you know what to do. You wanted to retire, so this is just icing on the cake, either take a bite or pass on it. You'll be fine, they want you, you don't need them." She kissed me on the cheek and we went in.

**

Chapter 27

An hour and a half later, we came out with a contract and Penny was the new host of "Vegas Alive" morning talk show, replacing the former host who was moving to Denver. She was holding in her excitement until we were out of the parking lot then she started screaming. I jumped when she did and smiled at her happiness. We went to see Lynn and Deacon at their precinct and they were thrilled that Penny was back to work.

"When do you start?" Deacon asked.

"I don't start taping until the first of next month so I have time to get ready. They're going to run a whole bunch of promotional spots about my moving from my old show to here. I have a good following of people that will be watching I'm sure. I called Gordy and he is arranging to see how many of my groupies, I mean my former staff; want to relocate here to work for me again. He's decided to move out also since I insisted he produce my show here too. The station people agreed."

"Well, we'll try to be in your studio audience for the first show." Lynn offered.

We talked a while longer but I was a bit fidgety about Lacey being alone at the house, so I said that we had to go check on our house guest. We all said our good-byes and left. Driving out to our home Penny was talking about the celebrities she wanted on her show. Penny reminded me of a teenager with a little magical power, waving her hand and making stars appear.

We arrived at the house and I saw a car parked on the shoulder of the road across from it. I asked Penny if she had her .38 and she said it was in her purse. I pulled into the drive, but drove the car down to the end of the garage over by where the guest house was. I couldn't see any movement in the small house and got out of the car telling Penny to be cautious and stay behind me.

We walked around the main house, between it and the guesthouse, to peek around the corner towards the pool. I didn't see anyone, no Lacey and no Willy. I was also concerned that I heard no alarms from our walking around the house. I went through the fence gate that prevented wild animals from entering the pool area and crept up along the back of the house, Penny right behind me. I peeked in the kitchen window over the sink that looked through into the living room, but saw nothing. If there were trouble, I would have figured by now someone would have seen us approaching the house. It was too quiet. I looked over to the pool and the ground was dry meaning no one had gotten out of the pool recently.

I moved up to the patio door just past the ugly statue, the sliding door was open, and I peeked into the dining area and beyond to the front vestibule, still nothing. I pulled out my cell phone and hit the speed dial for Lacey's cell phone and waited to hear the ringing. I could hear her phone playing it's little tune in the house but she didn't answer. I told Penny to stay at the door and I took a big breath and properly held my Glock out in front of me like the good cops do on TV and went in, moving my gun quickly back and forth watching for movement. I could hear Lacey's phone still ringing and went in that direction. As I was just coming around a corner, I suddenly realized that I had a gun stuck in the side of my face. I turned my head slowly and saw the man holding the gun, he didn't look friendly. He reached over and with his free hand took my Glock out of my hand. He quietly told me to put my hands out where he could see them and to call my wife to come in without her gun.

"Penny, I think you need to leave your gun outside and come in. I have a gun pointed at me right now and this guy doesn't look friendly," I said waiting to hear Penny move in, but I didn't. I turned my head towards the patio door and didn't see Penny at all. The guy came around me quickly and yelled for Penny to come in or she would be minus one husband.

I heard the click of a gun hammer being pulled back and turned my head to see behind the man, it was Penny. The man heard it also and turned quickly but Penny had fired, winging him in the gun arm, she just wouldn't kill anyone. I grabbed the man from behind and pulled him down yelling to Penny to be careful in case there was anyone else in the house. She looked down the hallway to see if anyone was coming out. I had taken my Glock back and was holding the man down with my knee. He was on his stomach, in pain and wasn't putting up much of a fight. I reached up and grabbed the long cord from the coffee maker and pulled it out of the socket and used it to tie his hands. I should have been in a rodeo; I had him tied in record time. I stood and picked up the man's gun and asked Penny how she did that.

Sin City Murders

"As soon as you went through the patio door, I went over and through your home office door by the pool and came around to see what was going on," she said proudly.

We cautiously walked down the hallway looking into Penny's spare room, no one there, and then to the guest bedroom and found Lacey gagged and tied up on the bed. I heard a yipping coming from the closet and figured Willy was inside. I opened the door and he came bounding out dancing around my feet. Penny was untying Lacey and she sat up with tears in her eyes. Penny was hugging her when I heard a crash back out in the house. I ran down the hall to find that the man on the floor had tried to move and pulled the coffee maker off the counter.

I stood looking at the mess he made when I was hit on the back of the head. I don't remember anything after that, but I woke in a van on the floor looking up to Penny and Lacey. The van was just pulling into a large building from what I could see on the floor, my head still spinning. I heard what sounded like a big overhead door closing and it was now darker than moments ago. I presumed we were in a big warehouse as I could see steel beams in the high up roof. The side door opened on the van, we were taken out and I found my feet, so they walked us to a door and into a hallway to another door. The three men stopped and one opened the door and pushed Penny, Lacey and me into the room.

It was an office, a very nice office. Carpeted in thick green plush reminding me of a lawn. The walls were covered in oil paintings and other objects of art on shelves. There was a carved desk that looked like maple and at the desk sat a very evil looking man. He had jet black hair slicked back by what could only be described as shiny grease, and a pencil thin mustache making him look like some silent movie star out of the twenties. He had a deep scar running from the corner of his left eye down to his neck; it was white against his tan skin. When he stood I could see he was tall and lean, he asked us to sit, pointing to the chairs in front of his desk.

"I'm sorry for the rough way you were brought here, but you interrupted the kidnapping I had hoped would go better. I just wanted the young lady, not the whole family." He grinned. "But you are all here and it may be better this way. All I need is information and you may provide it for me since you are in on the investigation, Mr. Richards."

"Well, you know my name, who are you?" I asked.

"I guess it doesn't matter, I am Artemis Merkins," he replied.

Sin City Murders

Penny spoke, "Isn't Artemis a Greek woman's name. The goddess of the hunt and the moon, twin sister to Apollo."

"Very good, Penny Wickens, you're smart as well as beautiful. Too bad you will have to die, such a waste. Mr. Richards, I can make your wife suffer terribly or kill her quickly, it's up to you. Just tell me everything you know that the police know about Muldoon and his morons, and what do they know about the operation that we have in place. I've managed to have all the flunkies killed off who screwed up the plan so far, it won't bother me to kill a few more people."

"Well, if you're going to kill us anyway, why should we tell you anything?" I said.

"I shall start by cutting off each finger of the ladies' hands, until you do talk. How does that sound to you?" He smiled evilly.

~~*~~

About ten minutes after we were taken away in the van, Buck pulled up to our home and saw my Crown Vic parked oddly off the side. The little voice in his head said that something was wrong. He went to the side of the house and around back figuring we'd be by the pool if everything as all right. He came around and found the patio door still open, going in to the kitchen he found the coffee maker broken on the floor. Now he was worried. He yelled for me and pulled his gun, searching the house, he found the ropes that had previously tied Lacey. Then he found Willy closed in the closet, not knowing that Penny had put him back in there so he'd be safe. Finding Willy in the closet definitely set off an alarm in his head so he pulled his cell phone and speed dialed Lynn explaining what he had found.

"All the cars are here and Jim would never leave the house open and go off, especially with the security turned off, and Willy is home alone, shut away in a closet." He spoke quickly.

Lynn said to sit tight and she would be out shortly with Deacon. She was calling a patrol car to come by also, she said and hung up. Buck walked around the house looking for any sign of what might have happened. He could smell gun powder so he figured someone had fired a gun recently. In the bedroom he found Penny's .38 on the floor and took a sniff, it had been fired. In the kitchen he saw blood on the floor by the spilt coffee, figuring Penny shot someone. He went out front and saw tire impressions in the ground by the porch, wide body tires, probably from a truck or van that must have pulled up to the front door to take away something or someone. About twenty minutes later two cars were flying up the road with flashers and sirens going. Lynn and Deacon got out of their car and came up to Buck, as he quickly explained what he had found.

Lynn looked pained, "Damn, I knew I should have put protection on them. This is not good."

**

Chapter 28

"So what could have happened?" Deacon asked.

"Well it's for sure they were taken, Jim would never have gone off with anyone and left the house in this condition." Buck said, holding Willy.

"All right, who could have taken them and where would they go?" Lynn asked.

"We know that Merkins is up to his ass in this, it's a good bet he has them." Deacon offered.

"From what I hear Merkins has an office right in the construction project of his casino-hotel, maybe they were taken there?" Lynn said.

"Well, let's go check it out?" Buck said.

"We can go check, but can't get inside to really see anything if we don't have a warrant, and we don't have enough probable cause for a warrant. No judge will issue a warrant on suspicion." Lynn said.

Buck thought a minute and said, "I have an idea." He moved back into the vestibule of the house and pulled his cell phone, made a brief call and came back out. "Now where is that office?" he asked.

A half hour later, Lynn and Deacon were parked in a public lot across Sahara Boulevard from the Merkins' casino-hotel construction project. Buck was standing at his car waiting for his men to drive up. "I'm going to take a few of my uniformed guards in and politely ask to see someone in charge about security jobs. I'll have the men suddenly go wandering off in different directions to confuse the people inside. Deacon should come along as a person looking for a little extra side job, so no warrant would be needed since he is with us as a civilian, in an unofficial capacity. Then we can explore the place to see where they might have our friends."

"We're skirting the law here, but it sounds good to me." Lynn said. "If you find out anything, call me and I'll have probable cause to enter as police." She had called for back-up while they waited. A van pulled up driven by Mac and five uniformed guards got out. Buck quickly explained what he wanted and they started across the road to the entrance of the building. Lynn and the back-up were hidden by the construction equipment in the lot as Buck, Deacon and the team went into the lobby of the office complex.

"May I help you?" The man at the reception desk asked. He looked more like a hired gun than receptionist, so Buck was careful what he said.

"Yes, we need to speak to someone in charge of security; I represent a guard company interested in subcontracting for the casino security." He told the man. The man just stared at Buck and his men and said he didn't think they would need guards yet. "Well, it doesn't hurt to talk to someone about it. Now if you could get on the phone and call, I'd appreciate it." While Buck was saying this his men were wandering around the lobby acting like they were just looking and some of them walked to the doors off the side and went in. The man at the desk was startled about this and asked if Buck could get his men out of there. Deacon said he'd go round them up and went through the door. Buck apologized for his men as the rest of the guards went through the door saying they would go get the other guards.

The desk guy was getting flustered and said they shouldn't be in there. Buck smiled as the man reached for a phone, then Buck put his big hand out to stop him. The man gave Buck a dirty look and went for a gun under his jacket, but Buck had already pulled his weapon and said "I wouldn't do that." He told the man to put the gun on the counter and to follow him, then they went through the door. Buck kept his gun low and asked the man where the offices of Merkins were. The man pointed down a hall and they went that way. Buck saw his men wandering in and out the various doors looking for anyone. Deacon came out of an office and Buck said while pointing, that Merkins' office was this way, so they went further down the hall.

They got to the door and Buck told one of his men to watch the receptionist as Deacon carefully opened the door and looked in. There was a waiting room and it was empty at the moment. Buck and Deacon went in followed by Mac and two guards. Deacon went to a door he figured was Merkins' office and opened it. He would apologize if he found it to be the wrong room or go blasting if it was right. He opened the door and the room was empty. He walked in with the rest of the men and stood looking around. Mac went to the huge floor to ceiling windows that overlooked the construction site for the buildings and suddenly made a yell. Everyone went over and looked out, they could see Merkins and his men leading Penny, Lacey and me from the from the building we were in, along the construction yard to a another building.

Deacon got on his cell and called Lynn saying they had spotted us, and needed help now. Buck was looking for a way to go to the yard, the building was confusing and he went back out to the hallway and grabbed the receptionist and asked him how to get out to the yard. The man was not talking but he looked towards a door off the side. Buck took it as an answer and sucker punched the guy, he went down. Deacon went to the door and pushed it open. It led to a stairwell leading down. Buck turned to his men and said he depended on them to help save his friends and not get hurt. They all went down and out a door to the yard, running now towards the building.

~~*~~

I was wondering how we would get out of this situation, I couldn't think very well while worrying about Penny and Lacey. Merkins led us to a room in the huge building that was still under construction. He ordered two of the three men he brought to tie up Lacey and Penny to a couple of ceiling bearing poles and told me to sit in a chair. I sat watching the women being tied and hoped something would happen soon, but what? No one knew we were here and I couldn't do anything but watch helplessly.

Merkins came to me and asked how much I knew about the investigation of Brantley's murder. I just sat wasting time as he told one of his men to take a blowtorch that was on a stand and light it. The man fired up the torch and I could see where this was going, I didn't like it. Merkins took the torch and gave me a smile and brought it up towards Penny.

"Okay! What do you want to know?" I yelled.

"Tell me everything you know that the police know." He said.

"Turn off the torch and I'll tell you."

He stood looking at me and slowly reached up and turned the control on the torch to the off position. He handed the torch to his man and came to me pulling a chair over. He turned it backwards and straddled it still smiling. "So talk."

"What do you expect from all this, killing a councilman and then murdering the men who set up the kill? Didn't you have enough to blackmail the other councilmen into voting for

the prostitution bill without killing Brantley?"
I asked.

He sat up and grinned, "I want everything
to go the way I want, if the bill doesn't pass
next week, its dead. They won't vote again, so I
have to be sure it passes. Brantley was a pain
in the ass, always spouting about the moral
obligation they had to the fine people of Vegas.
Screw those fine people; it's the tourists who
count, and their money. Muldoon had enough
information to blackmail a couple of
councilmen from their visits to his strip club
and the hookers they enjoyed, but it wasn't
enough to sway the vote in favor of passing. We
had to get rid of Brantley, so I had Muldoon set
up the murder in the motel to look like he died
screwing a hooker. Then we strong armed
Muldoon onto the council and the rest of the
story is how plans can go wrong when you hire
the wrong people to do the job. I need to know
what is going on to do some damage control. So
what do you know?" He folded his arms and
leaned on the back of the chair, waiting.

"I know if we disappear, there will be cops
looking at you closely. You're leaving too many
bodies, and the cops know from Mosh that
you're involved. They will be looking at you if
we turn up dead too."

"Oh, you won't turn up dead. I'm going to
have you put into the concrete supports

holding up the parking structure, a fitting monument for your illustrious career as a detective." He pointed at the windows to the giant cement machines pouring concrete into holes in the ground.

"Well, you haven't killed off everyone in your plan; Mason is still alive and is under protection. He's going to sing loud and if you hadn't heard, Mosh is still alive also. So you will need to cover your ass quickly."

Merkins look to his men and had a disappointed expression. He turned back to me and said, "Well, we will take care of that."

"Do you think you can take care of the entire Las Vegas police department? I have good friends with them and they won't rest till you are taken down." I said still stalling.

"Richards, you are boring me, now talk or I'll do something you'll regret." He stood and went to Lacey cutting her ties with a switchblade he whipped out. He pulled her to a table, putting down her hand palm up and held the blade over her fingers pushing down, she screamed, loud.

Deacon and Buck heard the scream and went in the direction it came from. They came to a door and burst through find Merkins, his men and us in the room. Merkins pulled up Lacey and held the knife to her neck. Merkins' thugs were running towards a back exit to get away from the men coming in the room with guns all drawn. Merkins was yelling to get back or he'd slit Lacey's throat.

I went to Penny and quickly untied her as Buck's men were approaching Merkins. I went towards him and said, "Don't be a fool Merkins, it's over now, kidnapping us and your plan has been recorded," I said as I pulled out my Palm Treo cell phone. "I had hit the record button earlier when I had a chance and recorded everything that went on from your office to here." He looked to me with hate and pulled Lacey back to a door and said not to follow him. He went through the door out into the yard where they were pouring cement for the foundation of the parking structure. Merkins didn't see Mac coming up behind him since Mac had gone a different way from the rest of the guards. He grabbed Merkins' arm that was holding the knife and pulled it from his hand and away from Lacey, then with his other arm he pulled Lacey away from Merkins.

Merkins turned and grabbed onto Mac as they struggled and fought. Mac punched Merkins with a blow that should have taken his head off but he just staggered back and then came up with another knife he pulled from a holder strapped above his ankle. Merkins took a couple swings at Mac and missed, Mac picked up a short cut two by four plank and swung it at Merkins connecting with his head, forcing Merkins to stagger back again, then he turned and walked into an opening in the ground where concrete was being poured. The construction workers were in a panic and pulled the concrete shoot away from the hole before it could fill. Deacon and Buck ran up as Mac stood looking into the hole about ten feet down but couldn't see Merkins.

The police had finally swooped in and the construction workers were still trying to dig out Merkins but the concrete had flowed faster than they could stop it. Lynn looked into the hole and said it's a fitting end to depravity.

**

Chapter 29

They finally did dig Merkins out, and he was dead. The ME had been in to pronounce time of death and cart his body off in the black bag. Merkins was in need of having cement chipped away from his body, I figured it would take the ME a few hours of chiseling.

Lacey was being treated by an EMT, Merkins had succeeded in cutting the tendons on two of her fingers, but maybe surgery would repair the damage; maybe, the tech said. Mac was sitting next to her with his arm around her and I was holding on to Penny, she was shaking a little but she would survive. She had been through worse.

Lynn came over and asked me to make a copy of the recording and give it to her when I could. I smiled and said, "Is it going to make a difference now that Merkins is dead?"

"Well, there are a lot of questions to be answered and we will need to go through all of Merkins' records to track down the rest of the investors in this scheme. This place may be grabbed up by one of the other casino corporations in town, it's a good location. The bill for the prostitution will probably fail now that the blackmail is off the table. You can give Mrs. Brantley the news that her husband's killers are all dead. I hope you are proud of yourself," she said with a laugh, and went off to explore Merkins office.

"Is this going to be our future now? No matter how many times I say we need to get away from murder and mayhem, it will follow us won't it?" Penny said as she was poking at my stomach now and I grabbed her hand and held it.

"Well, you have your new show to do now, so you will be away from most of my business. Besides, now you have a weapon to protect yourself better. Look, no matter where we go the curse will follow, but you're doing a great job of protecting me, you've already shot two men since we've been out here." She just gave me a big eyed stare, like I was a crazy person. I laughed and kissed her nose.

We went over to Lacey and Mac as they sat on the back of the EMS unit that pulled into the construction area. The construction workers were all given the rest of the day off by the supervisor after it was explained to him what happened. Lacey was sort of drifting from the pain killers the EMT had given her. Mac was worried and said they'd have to take her to the hospital but he'd watch her for a while till she felt better. I said I'd take care of the hospital bills, so tell them to contact me and I gave him my card.

I thought that Mac had a little crush on Lacey and vice-versa. I knew her fingers may never be the same if they couldn't fix the tendons back to normal. She may not be able to deal cards again, ending her career at the casino. I took Penny aside and told her this, then said, "I was thinking, maybe I could hire Lacey to work in the office, running accounts and writing paychecks for Buck's guards and keeping track of my clients. I think she'd do a good job."

"I was thinking the same thing; we're just always on the same wavelength aren't we?" She smiled. I looked over to Lacey and she was watching us, I called over to her, "Lacey, how would you like to come to work for me at the office?"

She smiled and said she'd love that and she asked, "Do I get to watch Willy too?"

Penny smiled and said, "He likes you, so you are his nanny now."

The EMT came back and said they were taking her in to look at the damage to her fingers. Lacey and Mac got up and went in the ambulance. Mac yelled to me about having someone take his van to the office and he would get there when he could. I said I'd tell Buck. The door was closed and the unit pulled out.

Penny and I went into the building where Merkins office was and found Lynn, Deacon and forensics going over the room. Lynn smiled and said the computer geeks had already found a number of accounts for investors in the Sin City project. Merkins wasn't very clever in hiding them.

Buck was lounging on the cushy couch in the office.

"Are you all worn out from your tough day?" I asked.

"Yep, this job can be a drag on an old body." He gave us his walrus smile.

"Old, you're younger than I am." I laughed.

"Age is all in the mind." He smiled again and Lynn came over with Deacon.

"Hey I forgot to ask, how did you find us?" I said.

"Thank Buck, he went to your house and called us when he saw there was a problem and he even figured out how to get us in this building without breaking too many laws." Lynn answered with a grin.

"I am a great detective." Buck smiled.

~~*~~

Penny was excited on the first day of her show. The station had gone all out to welcome her, even inviting the mayor of Las Vegas to present her with the key to the city. Lynn, Deacon, Buck, Maria, Lacey and Mac were standing off the side watching the start of the show. Lynn, Maria and Lacey were all excited that Penny's first guest was a well-known hunky actor who happened to be in town promoting his movie filmed in Vegas.

She did very well and the show went smoothly, she talked about the adventures we just went through since the media had gotten hold of the story, so they figured they may as well capitalize on it since she lived through it.

After the show we sat in Penny's new dressing room, her groupies were all there having been thrilled to move out to Vegas to give Penny her hair and make-up treatments. Gordy breezed in and said the station heads were ecstatic about the first show and they would have the ratings in tomorrow, but they were sure they would be good. He said Penny's face was all over town, on busses, billboards and taxi tops. He was bouncing off the walls, and said it was the best move she could have made. She didn't want to burst his bubble by saying he wasn't all in favor of her moving when they were back in Michigan. She just smiled and he went out.

Lacey and Mac came over to us and she said, "This last month has been wonderful, thank you for giving me a great job, I'll get used to all the craziness one of these days. I just want to say that Mac and I are engaged and when we do decide on a date to get married we would like you to be in our wedding party." She looked to me and asked, "I'd be honored if you'd give me away."

"I would be delighted. Mac, who is your best man going to be?" I asked.

He looked to Buck and said, "I asked Buck to fill in there."

"Wise choice." Buck said.

Lynn's cell phone rang and Penny looked to me. and said, "Don't even think about it."

I laughed and Lynn finished her call. "They got three of the outside investors under indictment for criminal activities backing up Merkins for the plot to turn Vegas into Dante's Inferno, which I found out was one of the names Merkins wanted to call his cat house. Since the prostitution bill didn't pass, the casino-hotel is going to be bought out by an east coast gambling consortium and built up as a new entertainment venue and casino. No hotel, just gambling and shows."

"Just what this town needs." I said, "By the way, whatever happened to Mason?"

"Don may have to do a small amount of time for his involvement in covering up the murder investigations, but he may get off with parole for helping to bring in the people who he knew were in on the deal. He had done a bit of investigating on his own into Muldoon's activities and found a whole lot of sleazy underworld goings on that he kept under wraps in case he needed it, and he did. For his testimony and the evidence he had, he may get off, but he won't be a cop again. Too bad."

"Did Mosh make it?" Penny asked.

"No, he expired about two weeks after he was poisoned. He didn't really fight it much, probably figured it was jail or death, so he took the easy way out."

We finished up at the studio, everyone going their own way and I drove Penny out to the strip and cruised up slowly as we admired the bright lights and happy people walking up and down the strip having a good time.

"I wonder how many people here are forgetting their troubles and problems and are just enjoying the moment?" I asked Penny and she smiled turning her head to me saying, "I hope they can keep that enjoyment in their hearts when ever those troubles rear their ugly heads. I know I will."

Willy was bouncing around in the back seat, Penny reached back and brought him up with us, he turned three times and then plopped down looking back and forth to us.

Penny was petting him and said, "I think it's time to go see Cher."

THE END

For every end there's a new beginning

Bob Moats

Preview from the twelfth book,
"Black Widow Murders"

Chapter 1

Harvey Trent was prone on his bed in the totally dark room when he felt them crawling on his chest. He had problems before with bed mites and had sprayed the mattress with some god-awful smelling spray that forced him to sleep on the couch for a week. The crawling continued and he was determined to ignore the damn bugs. Harvey told himself he was probably dreaming and to snub the minuscule creatures, they would go away, but they didn't. Then he suddenly felt something like a large feather brush over his chest, causing the tiny creatures to act agitated and then it happened, the first bite. Then a couple more, then a lot of tiny bites. Now he was feeling pain and a burning sensation, so he got up and went to the bathroom. He flipped on the light and turned to the mirror above the sink, what he saw almost made his heart stop. A dozen or so spiders were hanging on to his chest and stomach still biting.

He screamed and ran to the shower, turning on the spray and trying to brush the damn beasts off his body. He watched as a few went down the drain and managed to get most of them off of him in the stream of water. He batted at the ones still hanging on and finally flicked the last one off. He now was looking at the tiny welts that were forming from the bites and they were burning worse now.

He climbed out of the tub and did a quick drying with a towel, moving back to the mirror to see the red bumps were not going away. He knew he was in trouble as he looked closely to one of the spiders that had landed in his sink; it had a red lantern shape on its back, a Black Widow! He was feeling nauseous now and was becoming dizzy. The phone he thought, he needed help, so he staggered to the living room bouncing off the walls and fell at the table where the phone sat. He managed to push 911 and when the voice came on, he screamed, "I'm dying from spider bites, help!"

As he lay on the floor dying, a dark clothed figure stepped around him, closing the container that minutes before held the dozen tiny spiders. The figure put the container and a plume feather in a back pack and then took out a self-inking rubber stamp from the backpack and pressed it to Harvey's forehead, leaving an ink mark, then the person quickly left the house. Harvey never felt the ink stamp, he was dead.

It was now five in the morning and Joseph Lang, the Clark County-Las Vegas medical examiner, was trying to finish his sandwich just outside the house when Detective Lynn Carter along with her partner, both as a cop and at home, Deacon DeAngelo came up. "Hey Joey, whatcha got?" Lynn asked.

"Ham on rye with horseradish," he replied nonchalantly.

Lynn looked at him for a moment, "No, I mean what have you got for the crime scene?"

"Oh, guy died from spider bites," he mumbled as he chewed his food.

"Okay, why was homicide called in?"

"That's the fun part; he was murdered with spiders, Black Widows. Someone dumped a bunch of the buggers on him and they did their thing and bit him to death." He swallowed the last bite of the sandwich. "Now I can go back in." He crumpled the sandwich wrapper and put it in the pocket of his coat then walked to the entrance of the house.

Lynn stood there not moving and Deacon asked her, "Aren't you going in? I know you really hate spiders but I'm sure they have the crime scene secured."

She looked at him with a fear in her eyes that he had never seen before, even when confronting a gun toting madman. "One spider is bad; a bunch of spiders is not good. You go in and check it out; I'll wait here for you."

Deacon looked around the ground and said, "There's probably more spiders in this yard than there are in the house right now."

"You are a mean son-of-a-bitch." She said and forced her body to go forward into the house. She saw the body of the late Harvey Trent by the overturned coffee table, the phone still in his hand. He was totally naked and she bent down to see the red welts on his upper body. Joe Lang was checking the body. "I thought a Black Widow's bite wouldn't kill you right away." Lynn said.

Lang looked to her, "Well, one bite would take a short while to kill, but I counted fourteen bites, so you do the math."

Lynn straightened up on the number of bites, looking around for all those spiders. Lang could sense her tension and said, "All the spiders are gone, either washed down the drain in the tub or smashed by Trent here as he attempted to brush them off. Just my expert opinion."

That didn't help Lynn's tension. Deacon came up behind her and said her name causing her to jump. "Do you want to see the bedroom?" he asked.

"Yeah, sure, we can do that." They walked down the hall and Deacon could see that Lynn was looking all around, checking for attacks from spiders. He was trying not to make light of it, knowing she really hated spiders.

They did a quick check of the bedroom and didn't see much. "Has CSI been though this room?" she asked.

"Yep, about an hour ago," said Lang from the hallway as he was heading to the bathroom just off the bedroom. Lynn followed him in and they stood examining the sink to see the dead spider in the bowl. Lynn turned and went out after seeing the tiny creature, fearing it would come back to life and jump her.

Lang turned to Deacon still standing in the bathroom, "She doesn't like spiders does she?"

"Nope, I'm the one who has to kill the things if they get in our apartment. I hate them too, but not fear them like she does."

Lynn called to the ME while she was still looking around the living room, "So why do you assume he was killed by someone. Couldn't there have been a nest of them and they decided to attack?"

Lang was coming down the hallway again as she asked this. "I might have thought that too, but I decided he was murdered when I found this." He went to the body and turned the man's head so it faced upwards and Lynn could see the mark. She got closer and could see it was a Black Widow stamped on his forehead. Lang looked to her and said, "I'd say we have a killer."

~~*~~

Later in the morning, Penny was smiling at camera three as the stage manager signaled to her that her guest was ready. "Vegas, we have a treat this morning, that really funny entertainer, straight from his afternoon show at the Golden Nugget, comedy magician Magic Bob is going to be here live in a few moments." She went on about her guests for tomorrow, she was now having more celebrities willing to sign up for her show and she was thrilled. I was enjoying her happiness; it was good for me also. A happy Penny is a sexy Penny.

She finished the show and went to her dressing room finding me sitting in the make-up chair telling her staff about the crimes I solved in my brief career. She pushed at the chair causing me to stand, I kissed her and she sat to get her make-up removed. "Are you here to annoy or take me to a fabulous lunch at the Bistro?" She asked.

"I was thinking more along the lines of Sonic's." I gave her a smile and she stuck her tongue out at me. Her groupies worked on turning her into an ordinary everyday citizen of Las Vegas, removing her TV show face, but she still glowed in her street makeup.

The girls finished her make-up and I joked, "Can't you make her look like Sheena Easton?" She whacked my stomach and said to blow it out my ear. She stood and I went to pick up Willy from the couch where he was sleeping soundly. He looked dazed and licked my hand; I put him in his doggy purse and slung it over my shoulder. Penny hugged the girls and told them she was really glad they moved to Vegas to continue to do her make-up. Celeste said she was honored to be there and loved Vegas.

We left and went out into the blazing heat and quickly into the car. I flipped on the air conditioning and drove out of the parking lot. It was now just starting spring in the valley, but it was not like back in Michigan where the seasons were recognizable. It was now almost one hundred degrees out in the relentless sun. I wasn't complaining, I spent most of my time in air conditioned rooms. I did take Penny to Bistros for lunch and she was happy. Then we went to my office to find Lacey looking flustered. "I'm trying to get things organized and Buck keeps moving things on me." I said I'd talk to him and told her to organize the way she wants.

I went to talk with Buck and said, "Lacey is trying to run the front office, she's inexperienced at it so she has to learn, now leave her alone to set it up so she'll know where everything is."

Buck smiled, "I know, I was just messing with her."

"Well, quit it, she's young and I don't want her trying to commit suicide again." Referring to how we met her after she tried to kill herself because of a crime lord trying to set her up for murder. We solved the case but she was still fragile.

"Yeah, I guess I have a strange sense of humor. I'll be easier on her now." He smiled. "So any good cases coming up?"

"Nothing yet, I have more ads going out to the public but it will be a waiting process."

I heard the entrance door open since I installed a little bell on it and went out to see Lynn and Deacon in the lobby. Lynn looked to me and said, "Do you like spiders?"

**

Continued in the book...

~~*~~

Jim Richards Family of Readers

Thanks to the following people who are now part of the Jim Richards Family of Readers. They have read a book or more and enjoyed them. They all volunteered to be included in the list. If you are a fan of the books, send me your full name and you will be included in future books. Send your name to murdernovels@bobmoats.com to be added here and on the website.

* Achim Feifel * Al Norris * Alex Wheatley * Alexandra Delporte-Wilkinson * Amy Tapia * Andrea Bryan * Anne Shepherd * Arianda Sugar * Arlene Markowski * Ashley Augustus * Audra Hall * Barbara Hughes * Barbara Sammons * Barbara Schuler * Barbara Zirger * Beth Donohue Plenskofski * Betsy Childress * Beth Gibson * Bill Sandy * Bill Tornquist * Billie-jo Collie * Boni J Rychener * Carl Bishopric * Carla Lewis * Carole Henderson * Carolyn Conroy * Carolyn Riddle-Linington * Cassy Bailey * Chad Hudson * Charlotte L Duran * Cheryl L. Everett * Cindy Ackley Nunn * Cindy Valstad * Connie Bancroft * Corinne Kay O'Daniel * Dana Robbins Chuchran * Dana Wichita * Danielle Monique * Darren Heald * Dave Travers * David Wilkinson * DeAnn Jannereth * Deanna Miller * Deb Breuker Balbo * Debbie Carter * Debbie White * Deborah Fartuch * Deborah Gauze * Deborah Sullivan * Dee King * Denise Freeman * Diana Carver * Dixie Beck * Donna Gould * Donna Thompson * Donny Minter * Doris Kight * Eddie Moore

Sin City Murders

* Eric Walters * Felicia Annette Bradfield * Francine Menor * Gail Chesney * Georgiann Minster * George Conner * Greg Colucci * Hayley Rankin * Harold Garcia * Heidi Arnold * Irma Ranee Coy * Jacqueline Moss * Jan Kimball * Janice Schneider * Janice Spoor * Jennifer Redmond * Jessica Keown-Belous * Jim Beck * Jo Boguslaw * Jo Turner * Joanne Marie Turner * John Peiffer * John Wisbiski * Joseph Wauro * Joyce Stacy * Joyce Trifiletti * Judy Franklin * Judy Travers * Judy Padgett * Julie Heath * Junnahvee Benson * Karen Dahl * Karen Grams * Karen Higham * Karen Kaiser * Karen Meinburg Richwine * Karen Kirkman Parker * Karin Hawkins * Kathleen Donohue Roesing * Kathleen Riddle-Wolfe * Kathy Hinds Moore * Kathy Jones * Kathy Mitchell * Katie Benzler * Kay Burns * Kelly Garcia * Ken Boggs * Keota Rodriguez * Kiera Mccarthy * Kim Estes * Kitty Stolle * Kristie Sciler * Kirsty Stanton * LaLonnie Scallen * Larry Morris * Leann Parr * Lenora Scales * Leslie Marie Jackson * Linda Forester * Linda Ingle Cox * Linda Kennerö * Linda Magill * Lisa Bower * Liz Gibson * Lorraine Wiman * Loretta Alexander * Lynda Bowles * Lynette Lawrance * LuAnn Louttit * Manny Rothman * Marcia Gibson DeWitt * Marie Calder * Marlene Bryan * MaryLouise Kramp * Mary Lynn Gross * Megan Atkins * Meghan Hyden * Melody Cannavan * Michael Carruthers * Michael Vannoy * Michelle Burns-Mitchell * Michelle Pilcher * Micki Potter * Mike Moats * Mimi Baur * Myrna Hecht * Nadine Sutton * Natalie Quine * Neena Martin * O'Della Wilson * Pat Pollington * Pat Rohn * Patricia Jarmon * Patricia C Trezza * Patrick Barry * Paul Lawrance * Peggy Davis * Phyllis Bassett * Raylene Matheny * Rebecca Collins Besner * Renee Brumley * Reta Hanna * Reta Moats * Roberta Navarro-Harder * Sally Berneathy * Sally Hubler * Sarah Santos * Satka Nikc * Sharon E.

Bob Moats

Edwards * Sharon Mangini * Sharon McMillon * Sheena Rawl * Sherry Amstutz * Shirley Alvarez * Shirley Davies * Shirley Williams * Stacie Rowe * Stephanie Conner * Steve Cullen * Susan Haughton * Susan Hesse Adams * Susan Salomon * Suzan K Chase * Taisha Cullum * Tamara Moore * Tammy Castleberry * Tammy Lynn Wood * Ted Murphy * Terri Atkins * Terri Creech * Terry Raab * Tonia Rachael Riggs-Williams * Travis Fleury-Lopez * Twyla Gawlas * Val Brooks * Walt Munsel * Yvonne Isakson *

Thank you to all these wonderful people.

Thank you for purchasing this book. I hope you enjoy it as much as I enjoyed writing it for my faithful readers. Please feel free to email me to tell me what you thought about my stories. I love hearing from the readers. I can be reached at murdernovels@bobmoats.com thanks again!

*

REVIEWS

Reviews and word of mouth are among the best ways for authors like me to succeed. If you enjoyed reading this book, I would love if you left a review, even if it's only a sentence or two, on Amazon or Goodreads (see my author links below). Your reviews make all the difference and are appreciated in ways I could never express. Here is a review of one of my books that made my day:

> "This book is a MUST READ. I thoroughly enjoyed it. It takes you through every emotion - sadness, joy, anger, hate and back to joy. I could not put it down, wanting to see what emotion the author was going to spring on me next. Love the characters and can't wait for the author's next book."

Also, check out Diemme Black's other published books:
Strumming Me at https://amzn.com/B01E0LZ5OA
Inked My Life at https://amzn.com/B00JAG7AQW

Please visit and follow Diemme Black at:
https://twitter.com/diemmeblack
https://www.facebook.com/diemme.black
https://www.facebook.com/diemmeblackauthor
https://www.instagram.com/diemmeblack
http://amzn.to/2bxJyoz
http://bit.ly/goodreadsDB
http://www.diemmeblack.com